The Girl, the Guardian, and the Gate

Heather Primm

DEDICATION

This book is dedicated to my children, Kayleigh and Blake. This is for you. For all the fantastical stories told in the round at the supper table. For your love of magic, and girls who save the day with their big hearts and their quick brains. For inspiring me to tell stories in the first place. Love you forever.

CONTENTS

ACKNOWLEDGMENTS

My first heartfelt thanks must go to my parents, Sharon and Kirby Primm, who didn't look at me like I was crazy when I told them I was writing a book with a full-time job and two small children at home. Your support has meant everything to me. Huge thanks also go to Kim Fraser, one of my very first readers, whose enthusiasm and gentle suggestions absolutely made this a better book.

And finally, thanks to my husband, Rodrigo Dorfman, for listening to me read the book to him every night like a bedtime story so that I could hear the flow of the narrative through his ears, and for encouraging me to send this, my first literary baby, out of the nest to fly free in the world. It's you and me, love, wherever our adventures might take us.

CHAPTER 1
THE LONGEST AFTERNOON

Annie Albright checked the clock above the whiteboard for possibly the hundredth time that afternoon. Twelve more minutes before the bell rang, which she was pretty sure was what the clock had showed the last time she looked. Either she was losing her mind, or time had actually slowed down. She thought both were real possibilities.

This was usually one of her favorite classes; science was her best subject after math, but today Ms. Trudy had made the mistake of asking Jay a question, which of course Jay knew the answer to.

Jay had been Annie's best friend since the first day of kindergarten, when they had shown up at school wearing matching Star Wars t-shirts. It was now their first year of middle school, and they had finally ended up in the same class again. There was no one Annie loved more in the entire world, except for her parents and, sometimes, her little sister Maisy. But even Annie could live without one of Jay's famous lectures on pretty much any subject, especially right at the end of the day.

"...the life cycle of a dragonfly only has three stages, unlike the beetle, which has four. But most of that life cycle takes place under water," he was saying, as he pushed his habitually floppy bangs out of his eyes.

Ms. Trudy's second mistake? Letting Jay keep talking long after he'd answered her original question.

They had been working on their life cycle project for weeks now. It was Jay's dream assignment – he even tried to get her to collect "specimens" on the playground at recess. For extra credit. Like she was going to pick up some random bug and carry it around in her pocket for the rest of the day.

She looked at the clock again. Seven minutes to go. Annie put her head down on her desk and closed her eyes.

As Jay continued to explain how the adult dragonfly came out of the water at the end of the nymph stage, she could hear the class behind her starting to get restless, shifting in their seats and rustling papers and books on their desks.

Someone in the back of the room coughed, loudly. Jay paused briefly, and then continued.

"If the nymph stage happens when it's cold outside, the dragonfly will actually wait in the water until it gets warm enough to come out. Then it climbs up onto a plant and sheds its skin."

Slam! Annie banged her head on the desk as she quickly sat up. Jay finally stopped talking, also looking startled.

"Oops, sorry about that," said a high, girlish voice from behind her.

Annie turned around. Ashley Keith was picking her science book up from the floor. She was smiling, but in a way that was not the least bit friendly. The rest of the class burst out laughing.

Ashley and her brother Beau were twins. They had transferred to Annie and Jay's school just a few weeks before from another middle school in the district. They were small for their age, with round, wide-eyed faces and dark blonde hair. Annie had heard one of the teachers say that they looked like angels. They definitely didn't act like them, though. Rumor had it that they had been expelled from pretty much every school in the county, and that this was their last chance to finish up sixth grade. If half of the stories she had heard were true, their next stop was probably a juvenile detention center.

Annie glanced across the aisle at Jay. The twins had been making fun of him regularly since they arrived, and they had been particularly obnoxious today. It was obvious to Annie at least that Ashley had dropped her book to interrupt Jay's speech, but as usual he seemed completely clueless, and appeared to be only waiting for the laughter to die down so he could continue.

"All right, everyone, that's enough," Ms. Trudy raised her voice to be heard over the still-snickering class. "Jay, thank you very much for that wealth of information. The rest of you," and here she looked sternly in Ashley and Beau's direction, "would benefit from spending as much time as Jay does on his homework."

"Yeah, but unlike Jay, I've actually got better things to do," Ashley said, in a voice that was just quiet enough that Ms. Trudy couldn't hear her from the front of the classroom. Annie frowned. She could tell that Ashley's words had bothered Jay – the tips of his ears always got red when he was upset. She tried to get his attention, but he was focused on Ms. Trudy, who was writing that night's assignment on the whiteboard, and he wouldn't look in her direction.

When the bell finally rang, Annie gathered up her things and said goodbye to Jay, who had recovered enough from Ashley's nasty comment to give her his usual cheery grin. She did notice that his ears were still a little red, though.

Slinging her backpack over her shoulder, she headed down to the office. Annie's father managed the computer networks for the entire district, so when he had to be at her school in the afternoons, she would usually catch a ride with him. She loved those days, because she got his undivided attention without constantly being interrupted by her sister. Nobody gets a word in edgewise with a four-year-old in the car.

"Anything exciting happen today?" her dad asked, checking over his shoulder as he backed out of his parking space.

"Not really," she replied. "Well, Jason Ellis threw up all over his desk after lunch. I guess that was kind of exciting. Gross, but exciting."

Her dad chuckled as he pulled up behind a caravan of school buses. "Still working on your life cycles project with Jay?"

That was a perfect lead-in if she'd ever heard one. What had happened in science class that afternoon was bothering her, a lot, and she was really hoping her dad could give her some advice about what to do. There had always been a handful of kids at school that Annie wasn't crazy about, but until the twins arrived there hadn't been anyone she would have called a bully. The twins definitely fell into that category, and Annie didn't see how Jay, who hated conflict unless it was a competition over grades, was going to be able to get them to leave him alone without her help.

It took most of the ride home to tell the story. Her dad was quiet as he pulled into their garage, unbuckled his seat belt and turned to face her.

"Listen, kiddo," he said, and Annie thought he sounded a little sad. "This is something Jay has to figure out for himself. It's one thing to stick up for your friend, and you should do that. But you can't fight his battles. If you're always there to do it, he'll never learn how to take care of himself. Does that make sense?"

Annie nodded to show she had heard, but she wasn't optimistic about that. Besides, that wasn't how it worked in any of the stories she read. In books, there was always somebody who knew what to do when people were in trouble. In books, there was always a hero.

CHAPTER 2
THE QUESTION

Annie was reading in bed that night when her mother came in with a pile of laundry, kicking aside toys so that a narrow strip of carpet became visible, like a runway leading to the door.

"Mom," Annie said, "can I ask you something?"

Annie's mother smiled as she tucked a pair of socks into the dresser drawer. This had always been Annie's favorite stalling technique at bedtime, hitting her mom with a particularly tricky question like why it never snows in Florida, or why snakes don't have noses.

"You've told me before that you had bullies at your school when you were a kid," Annie said. "How do you get them to leave someone alone?"

Her mother stopped folding shirts and looked at her.

Annie had been thinking all evening about what her dad had said in the car. It didn't seem fair to her to leave Jay to figure out how to handle the twins on his own. This was one of those times that Annie wished real life was more like a book, and that she was a hero like the ones in the adventure stories she loved.

Of course, Annie wished that most of the time. She and Jay might not always see eye to eye on bugs, but one thing they did share was a love of books, especially fantasy and science fiction. She was pretty sure that between them they had read everything in that section of the media center, and the librarian had finally started directing them to books well beyond their grade level. If it had dragons, goblins, robots or aliens, they had probably already read it. While a lot of the other kids her age seemed to spend most of their time in front of a screen, Annie would much rather read, because it allowed her to "see" the characters the way they looked in her imagination.

Annie's mother sat down on the edge of the bed, the shirt she had been folding still in her hands. "Is this about what happened with Jay today at school?" she asked.

"Yeah," Annie said dejectedly. "I don't know, I just wish it was as easy to solve problems in real life as it is in stories. Not exactly easy," she amended, "but at least the heroes always seem to know what to do."

Annie's mother brushed her hair out of her eyes. "I hear you," she said. "But the world we live in is a little more complicated. Even the people you would consider real life heroes would likely tell you they aren't always sure of themselves. What makes them heroes isn't that they always know what to do, it's that they never stop trying. Does that make sense?"

"I guess," Annie said, reluctantly. "But I'd rather be the other kind of hero. It sounds like a lot more fun."

Annie's mother laughed. "I hear you on that, too. That's exactly why people write those kinds of stories, and why people read them. It's wonderful to be able to escape into a book like that, especially when you have problems you feel like you don't know how to solve."

Annie's mother glanced over at the clock on the desk and smiled. "It's time for bed, I'm afraid," she said, taking Annie's book and placing it next to the clock. "We can talk about this some more tomorrow. Try not to worry. Jay doesn't need you to be a hero. He just needs you to be his friend."

After her mother left, Annie rolled over onto her side, tucking Miss Kitty, her favorite stuffed animal, under her arm. In the moments before sleep overtook her, still mulling over what her mother had said, she muttered into the darkness, "Why can't I be both?"

CHAPTER 3
THE COUNCIL CONVENES

Hours later, the house was quiet except for the usual nighttime noises — crickets chirping in a constant, steady rhythm, the whisper of the ceiling fans. Annie's alarm clock hummed softly on the brightly painted schoolhouse desk that had once belonged to her grandmother.

The silence was broken by a faint rustling sound from the bookcase in the corner of the room. If anyone had been awake to hear it, they might have mistaken it for the scrabbling of a small animal inside the walls, or the shifting of the floorboards as the old house settled in for the night.

But, if anyone had been watching the bookcase in the darkness, they would have spotted the source of the noise immediately. Dozens of bright, blinking eyes peeked out from the crevices formed on the shelves between oddly shaped books. A few moments later the owners of those eyes crept out from the shadows, flinching in the moonlight that spilled across the floor. Tossing remnants of yarn from one of Annie's art projects like ropes, they rappelled down the side of the bookcase with the ease of mountain climbers, dropping noiselessly to the carpet below.

There were approximately twenty of them in all, and the largest stood no taller than the wooden people in Annie's dollhouse, collecting dust at the foot of the bed. It was in this dollhouse that they gathered, crowding into the tiny rooms and bumping into furniture in their haste to assemble.

They looked out of place in the dollhouse, but truthfully, they would have looked out of place almost anywhere. A mermaid slithered awkwardly across the braided rug on the floor. A medieval knight sitting stiffly on an embroidered sofa poured something that smelled like nail polish remover into a tiny teacup and drank it down in one gulp. A centaur sent a chair clattering to the dollhouse floor with a swish of his elaborately braided tail.

As the mermaid hissed angrily at the careless centaur, who was awkwardly trying to pick up the fallen chair with his forelegs, a figure stepped forward from the shadows, leaning heavily on a wooden walking stick. She cleared her throat, and silence fell immediately.

She was even smaller than the others, and very thin. Her hands were gnarled but oddly delicate, like bundles of twigs bound together by string. She had snow white hair that fell loosely down her back, and her face was heavily lined with age. The flowing brown dress she wore was so close to the color of her skin that it was difficult to see where one left off and the other began.

"I am glad to see you found the way," she said, smiling at the others in greeting. No cemetery could have been quieter than that room as they waited for her next words.

"She is ready," the old woman said.

Excited muttering broke out immediately, but the room quieted when the old woman tapped her cane gently upon the floor.

"It is time," the old woman continued, "to choose her guardian."

The crickets chirped loudly outside the window, and the cat played chase with his tail on the other side of the door. But inside Annie's room there was absolute silence. No one moved. No one spoke. The crowd held its collective breath.

Finally, a young woman stepped forward. She wore a dress of forest green velvet, almost exactly the shade of the hissing snakes that wreathed her head like living hair.

"A thousand pardons, Lady," she said, in a voice like truck tires on a gravel road. "but she is so young. Are you absolutely sure she is ready?"

The Lady nodded. "It is true that she is very young. But age is not always the best indicator of wisdom. She believes she is ready, and so she is."

She folded her hands over the top of her walking stick and waited. After a long pause, there was a flicker of movement at the very back of the room. It rippled like a wave through the assembled group until finally those at the front stepped to either side, staring in astonishment at the creature now standing in the dim halo cast by Annie's nightlight. He addressed the old woman in a tiny, trembling voice.

"I will do it."

There was another long moment before anyone reacted at all, followed by an explosion of riotous laughter, so loud that Annie shifted restlessly in her sleep. The Lady raised her hand for silence, her eyes never leaving the speaker's face.

His appearance was not as fierce as some of the others, but it was certainly as odd. He was a rabbit, with soft grey fur and ridiculously long ears. His whiskers drooped slightly at the ends, as if pulled gently downward by invisible fingers. He wore black buccaneer boots on his large feet, and a felt patch over his left eye. A quiver of arrows and a wooden bow were strapped to his back, the weight of which threatened to tip him over. He was visibly shaking.

"I will do it," he said again, and this time his voice was slightly stronger.

The old woman regarded the rabbit seriously. "Why do you volunteer, Grimsley?"

"I have watched her longer than any other Guardian," he responded quietly, "and loved her longer, too." He looked around defiantly as if expecting to be contradicted, but no one spoke.

"I am not afraid," he said, though he was clearly terrified, "I can do this." He seemed now to be speaking for the old woman's ears alone, "I know I can. Please."

She must have seen what she needed to see in his determined face, because she smiled at him before turning to address the crowd.

"It is decided," she stated firmly. "Grimsley will be her Guardian. The rest of you will provide assistance however it is needed."

The others nodded in agreement, although they looked a bit stunned.

The meeting came to a close as sunlight began to bleed around the edges of the curtains. One by one the Guardians left the dollhouse. Eventually, only the rabbit and the old woman remained.

Grimsley gazed up at the bed where Annie lay sleeping, his one eye huge and liquid in the semi-darkness. The Lady's expression softened as she looked at him, frozen in place by the enormity of the decision he had made.

"Try not to be afraid," she said, kindly. "You were born for this task, and while I cannot promise you that there will never be challenges, you will never be alone."

She smiled, placing her gnarled, bony hand over his paw. Then she simply disappeared, there one minute and gone the next, like something you only thought you had seen with your eyes half open in the dark.

Grimsley let out a deep breath and began to climb down the side of the dollhouse towards home.

CHAPTER 4
THE GARDEN

The next day at school passed uneventfully. The twins had been absent, probably in detention as they so often were, so the worst thing that happened was that Jay had gotten a score that was four points higher than hers on the math test Mr. Walliford handled back. Annie was grateful, as she still didn't have any idea what to do to help her friend.

After supper that night, she cruised the neighborhood on her bike, but everyone seemed to already be in for the night. Back at home her parents were watching some old TV show that used to be on when they were kids, giggling quietly to each other over jokes that made absolutely no sense at all. She tried to play Old Maid with Maisy, who kept throwing her cards across the room whenever Annie got a match. Eventually she gave up and went to her room to curl up with Miss Kitty and a book her mom had picked up for her at the library.

She woke hours later in a dark, quiet room. Looking out her window at a star-scattered sky, she realized that she must have fallen asleep. Her mother had obviously come in at some point, because her book lay closed on the bedside table and the blankets had been pulled up to her chin. Comfortable and sleepy, she burrowed under the covers and closed her eyes.

When she opened them again, she knew immediately that she was dreaming. Instead of flannel sheets, she was lying on a patch of flowering green moss, soft as velvet against her skin. The sky was bright with morning sunlight, and a gentle breeze ruffled her hair.

She sat up quickly and looked around. She was in a garden, but it was unlike any she'd ever seen before. The gardens in her neighborhood were neat little boxes lined with rows of flowers in coordinating colors. This was so different that it almost didn't seem right to call it by the same name.

First of all, it was enormous, about the size of her back yard, and surrounded on all sides by a high stone wall, crawling with ivy. At each corner stood a crenellated tower, like a castle in a fairy tale.

The flowers didn't look much like the ones she was used to, either. There were no roses, daisies, or petunias here. Instead there were purple bell-shaped flowers twice as tall as she was, drooping from spindly stems like drinking straws. Tiny blossoms shaped exactly like little mouths rose just inches from the ground, forming a carpet of vibrant blue. The sunflowers she recognized at least, but she had never seen them as big as satellite dishes before.

Every inch of the ground was covered. It looked like a bomb had gone off in a florist's shop and things had taken root wherever they had landed. In fact, the only place to put her feet was a narrow cobblestone path that wound through the garden, beginning at the outer wall and circling in increasingly tighter loops towards the center. It ended there, at a cluster of trees so heavy with vibrant pink flowers that their weight pulled the branches down to brush the ground like the tail feathers of some exotic bird.

It was the most beautiful place she had ever seen.

She followed the path to the brilliant pink trees at the center of the garden. Parting the branches like curtains, she found herself in a small clearing. The ivy had grown up the tree trunks here, forming a tangled canopy of green that blocked out all but occasional rays from the sun overhead. What little light did break through dappled the leaf-strewn floor, dimly illuminating the small stone bench at its center, and the creature that sat upon it, talking quietly to himself.

CHAPTER 5
THE GUARDIAN

"This is the weirdest dream I have ever had in my life."

He jumped when she spoke, reaching behind his back for a beautifully carved wooden bow. Startled, she quickly ducked behind the nearest tree.

When no arrow came whistling by, Annie risked a peek around the tree trunk. At the sight of her, the creature's eyes widened, and his shoulders slumped forward. He lowered the bow with trembling paws, and sat down hard on the stone bench, closing his eyes. He began to rock back and forth, like her little sister when she was tired and didn't want to go to bed.

Normally Annie would have been a bit concerned about an unexpected encounter with a giant rabbit; especially one that was wearing pirate's boots and an eye patch. But, as this was a dream, she didn't think it was likely that he'd be able to hurt her.

Besides, the rabbit seemed familiar somehow. Looking at him made her feel strangely safe. She crossed to the bench and sat down beside him.

"Um," she began. "Hi, I guess? My name's Annie. What's yours?"

The rabbit's entire body was trembling. With fear? Excitement? Both?

She waited for him to respond. She was pretty sure he could talk, having heard him muttering to himself when she first entered the clearing. After a few minutes she decided he wasn't going to answer her, and she stood up.

"Okay, you're obviously not in the mood to talk," she said. "If you change your mind, I'll be out in the garden."

She had only gotten about three steps when she heard a soft voice behind her.

"I am called Grimsley, Miss Annie," the rabbit said. "That has been my name since the day you imagined me."

"What?" She turned sharply around, shocked by his sudden speech as much as the words themselves. "I did what?"

He rose from the bench and took a tentative step forward.

"You imagined me," he repeated, quietly.

"That doesn't make any sense," Annie was completely confused. "I don't even know who you are."

He shivered, as if the temperature had suddenly dropped. Instinctively, she took his paws in her hands and gently pulled him back to the bench. At her touch, his trembling subsided at once. He took one deep, shuddering breath, and he began to speak.

"Every child is given the gift of imagination at birth." His words came slowly, as if he chose each one with care. "Some use it only while they are young, abandoning it entirely when they are grown. Others choose never to use it at all, and it withers and dies within them.

But there are some children," he gave her a timid smile, "who recognize this gift for what it is - magic. These children don't just use their imaginations, they feed them."

"I'm sorry," said Annie, and she really was, because he looked so earnest, "but I still don't understand."

"You are one of those special children, Miss Annie. From the time you were old enough to be aware of it, you have fed your imagination. While the other children your age watched television, you read stories. While they played video games, you daydreamed. You have imagined whole worlds in the quiet moments that other people fill with meaningless activities for fear of boredom. You imagined me," he said, shyly, "because of a story you once loved."

Annie stared at him, racking her brain. Suddenly, she realized why he looked so familiar. Reaching out slowly so she wouldn't frighten him, she touched one of his velvety grey ears. She closed her eyes and the memory rolled over her like a wave. The last present she opened on Christmas morning the year she was five; a book, and the little stuffed rabbit that came with it.

The story was about the youngest brother in a family of rabbits, who was afraid of everything. His brothers and sisters teased him mercilessly and went off to have adventures while he stayed at home, too timid to join them. He was so frightened of the world that he spent his days building a fence around their hidey-hole to keep it at bay.

One day the rabbits encountered a hungry fox in the meadow, and he chased them all the way home. Only the fence their brother had built kept them from being eaten, as they escaped behind it in the nick of time.

It was kind of a creepy story for a little kid, now that she thought about it, but oh, how she had loved that stuffed rabbit. She had slept with it for years, until its fur had worn thin from her affections.

"I do remember you," she said, as she reluctantly removed her hand from his ear. "But, in my book you never wore boots. Or an eye patch. And you definitely didn't have a bow and arrows."

"As your imagination grew and changed, so did I," he explained.

She thought about the kinds of books she had been reading since the year she discovered Harry Potter, and some of the daydreams she'd had. He was probably lucky not to be wearing a jetpack.

"I have been shaped by many stories," he continued, "but I was born with that first one, so it remains the biggest part of who I am."

The feeling that she had known him forever intensified. She had to restrain the urge to put her arms around him and hold him the way she had held her stuffed rabbit.

"What is this place, anyway?" she asked. "I understand where you came from, but I've never seen anything like this garden before."

The rabbit slapped one paw against his forehead in a strangely human gesture.

"Oh!" he cried, "I had completely forgotten!"

With a funny little sideways jump, he kicked off one of his high black boots and began rummaging inside it like a suitcase.

After discarding a peculiar variety of items, including a yo-yo, a boomerang, and one of those little umbrellas that adults put in their drinks at parties, he withdrew a scroll of yellowish paper. It was tied together with a length of gold ribbon that glittered in the weak rays of sunlight peeking through the trees.

Still wearing only one boot, he stood up and unfurled the scroll, which pooled on the ground at his feet. She could see words through the thin paper, a sprawling cursive that filled every inch except for the narrow margins.

The rabbit pulled himself up so that his back was ramrod straight, held the scroll at arm's length, and began to read.

"Greetings to you, Anneliese Marie Albright, from the Council of Guardians. I am here to escort you to Bibylonia."

CHAPTER 6
THE GATE

Annie had never had a dream like this one before, with places and creatures she'd never seen before. It felt a lot more like something you would read in a book; certainly it was more exciting than her usual dreams, where she couldn't remember where she lived, or she forgot to do her homework for an entire year. It felt so real, too. Annie could swear she could smell the flowers tumbling down around them from the vines that hung over the clearing.

"What's the Council of Guardians?" she asked.

"We are responsible for protecting the garden," he said simply, as if that explained everything.

She raised one eyebrow at him, a trick she and Jay had been practicing for the past three weeks. She must have managed it this time, because Grimsley hastily continued.

"The garden is the way your imagination looks when it is given form. It is the bridge between your world and ours."

"And what is your world?" Annie asked. "This Bibylonia place you were talking about?"

Grimsley stepped out of the clearing, and Annie followed. He pointed towards an enormous iron gate set into an opening in the stone wall.

"Bibylonia lies just beyond the gate, through the forest."

They began to walk towards it. As they grew closer, Annie spotted flickers of movement in the trees on the other side. She knew this was just a dream, but excitement sent her heart racing anyway. What was on the other side of that wall?

In the center of the gate was an ornate, old-fashioned lock. It shone more brightly than the rest, as if someone had just polished it and scurried away before they could be seen. It made her think of the old house they had lived in briefly when she was six and her mother's job had taken them to Tennessee for the summer. All the doors had glass knobs that looked to Annie's young eyes like huge diamonds, and they opened with something called a skeleton key, old-fashioned and toothed like a jack-o'-lantern.

As she turned back to Grimsley, she found him holding a key that looked very much like the one they had used in that house. It gleamed brightly, like the lock itself, and it dangled from a beautiful silver chain.

"This is for you, Miss Annie," Grimsley held it out to her.

She took it from him eagerly and was already reaching towards the gate when a sudden warning chimed in her brain. She pulled her hand back quickly and turned to the rabbit, folding her arms across her chest.

"Okay," she said. "What are the rules?"

He blinked.

"Listen," she said, "I read these kinds of stories all the time. There are always rules."

She held up a hand and began ticking them off on her fingers. "Make sure you're gone before dark. Don't eat the food because then you'll have to stay forever. Don't tell anyone your real name. Then there's my personal favorite - time passes differently, so don't stay too long or you'll be gone from your own world for a hundred years. So, before I put one foot into this Bibylonia of yours, I need to know the rules."

Grimsley smiled, a little sheepishly.

"My apologies, Miss Annie. I'm afraid that the excitement of actually speaking with you seems to have scattered my brain."

He cleared his throat before continuing. "First," he said, "you must be escorted at all times by your Guardian, who is appointed by the Council."

"Er," he said, ducking his head. "That would be me."

"You may eat and drink as you like, and there is no creature in Bibylonia that does not already know your name. But time does indeed pass differently. Once you open the gate, whatever time you spend on the other side will fall within the hours that your world lies sleeping.

Finally," he suddenly became serious, "you must keep your key with you always. The gate must remain locked except for when you enter and depart. This is the most important rule of all. No creature outside of the Council is allowed to enter the garden, and nothing from your world may enter ours, except for you and your talisman, of course."

"My talisman?" she asked. She had heard that word before. "Isn't that a medal you wear around your neck to ward off evil or something like that?"

He sighed. "Another thing I have forgotten to tell you. I really should have made a list.

A talisman," he explained, "is something that brings you luck, or protects you. It should be the thing that you would most want with you if you were afraid or facing danger."

Annie thought about it. She had an excellent slingshot that her grandmother had given her, and that her mother refused to let her play with except at her grandmother's house. She also had a "magic" wand that she suspected might end up actually being magic in this crazy dream. But…

"It can be anything?" she asked. "Anything at all?"

"Yes, Miss Annie," he confirmed.

In the end, it was an easy decision to make. There were probably a dozen items in her room that would be more helpful in a dangerous situation, but there was just one thing she always looked for when she felt vulnerable, sad, or afraid; it always made her feel like everything was right with the world again. She closed her eyes and concentrated as hard as she could. When she held a perfect image of her talisman in her mind, she opened them again.

For a few moments, he looked like he always did, a fluffy black ball of fur with a streak of white down his back that made him look more like a skunk than the overweight housecat he was. But, as Annie watched, Marty began to change. His back stretched like an accordion, and his legs lengthened with comical speed, so that for a moment he looked like a cat on stilts. His muzzle widened, and his tiny belled collar seemed to expand briefly with his thickening neck before it snapped and fell limply to the ground.

When the metamorphosis was complete, it was a fully-grown Bengal tiger that bounded over to Annie and rolled onto his back at her feet, obviously hoping for a belly rub. She crouched beside him and ran her hands through his fur. He butted her rib cage with his huge head and knocked her down, where he attempted, unsuccessfully, to climb into her lap.

She burst out laughing, holding onto the cat's shoulder for leverage as she pulled herself up.

Grimsley was halfway up the gate, staring down at the tiger in terror.

"He won't hurt you," Annie promised. "He doesn't even eat tuna fish, so I'm pretty sure he wouldn't like rabbit. Why did he turn into a tiger, anyway?"

"I am not precisely sure, Miss Annie." His voice was so high that she was pretty sure all the bats in a five-mile radius had just covered their ears. "But the garden is a place where what is imagined becomes possible. My best guess," Grimsley said with an audible gulp, "is that he is a tiger here because he believes himself to be a tiger."

Marty reared up on his back legs to put his paws on her shoulders, knocking her down again. "Okay, okay," she laughed, "I get it. You're glad to see me."

She called up to the rabbit again. "You can come down from there. I promise I won't even let him lick you."

He didn't look happy, but he began to inch slowly down the gate. Marty ignored him completely in favor of chasing his enormous new tail in endless

16

circles.

She squinted into the sunlight, trying to see what lay beyond the forest on the other side.

"What's out there?"

Grimsley had reached the ground. Placing his large paw gently over her fingers, he closed her hand around the key.

"You will know it when you see it, I think," he said. "After all, you imagined it."

Unable to wait any longer, she fitted the key into the lock. The door creaked open, and through a gap in the trees she caught her first glimpse of Bibylonia beyond the edge of the forest.

Waiting.

For her.

CHAPTER 7
ON THE BEATEN PATH

Marty bumped her legs affectionately with his massive jaw as she pushed open the gate. Remembering Grimsley's instructions, she turned and locked it behind them, slipping the key on its long silver chain around her neck for safekeeping.

They were in a forest, older than any she had ever seen outside of books. She knew it was old because the trees were so huge that her house would have fit comfortably in the branches of the smallest one.

Leading away from the gate was a dirt path, just wide enough for the three of them. It snaked through the forest like a river and disappeared from view in the thick of the trees.

"Not exactly the yellow brick road, but it works," she muttered to herself.

As she stepped onto the path, she felt a great gust of air rise up from the ground, sending little cyclones of dirt spinning around her ankles. The wind rose higher, lifting her short brown hair and whipping it around her face. Then, just as suddenly, it stopped, and the dry leaves scratching her legs began to settle at her feet.

"Well, that was a little weird," she laughed. "I guess I know what it feels like to go through the dryer now."

She looked down to assess the condition of her pajamas and her laughter died in her throat.

Instead of the ratty old t-shirt and shorts she had gone to sleep in, she was wearing a dark green tunic that fell almost to her knees, cinched at the waist with a wide brown leather belt. Hanging from the belt was a small cloth pouch, tied with a drawstring. Beneath the tunic she wore velvet-soft leggings patterned with autumn leaves. Her feet fit perfectly in slouchy ankle boots the precise shade of the forest floor. She pushed her hair out of her face and discovered that it seemed to have grown a foot since she opened the gate; it now hung loosely down her back instead of barely brushing her shoulders.

She had definitely had strange dreams before, but freak windstorms and total wardrobe changes were a little out of the ordinary. And while the clothes weren't things she would have picked out for herself, she had to admit she liked them. The leggings would be easy to move in, the tunic was warm without being uncomfortable, and the long hair was pretty cool, even if it wasn't very practical. If only she had something to pull it back with, so it wasn't all over the place.

She examined the pouch hanging from her belt, thinking she could possibly use the drawstring that was holding it together to tie back her hair. When she pulled at the string to see if it could easily be removed, the pouch opened at her touch, revealing a comb, a thin leather cord just the right length for the end of a braid, and a small round mirror. She combed the snarls out of her hair and braided it quickly over one shoulder. When she had finished, she tucked the comb back into the bag and pulled out the mirror. Holding it up, she got her first good look at her transformation.

"Whoa." she said, and for a few long moments that was all she could manage. She still looked like herself: the same hazel eyes and light brown hair, same spattering of freckles across the bridge of her nose. But she looked different too. Older, maybe. Like someone that interesting things happened to.

Grimsley and Marty hadn't changed at all. Apparently, their current forms were appropriate for whatever this world had to offer. Grimsley was still eyeing the tiger warily, and the tiger still seemed completely unaffected by the presence of the rabbit.

She laughed and took Grimsley by the arm.

"Come on, boys," she said, to her former housecat and her newfound friend. "Let's see what's out there."

CHAPTER 8
A BRAND-NEW WORLD

Trying to describe Bibylonia would be nearly impossible, Annie thought. They first emerged from the forest at the edge of an immense mountain range, dotted with snowcaps and tall, leggy pine trees. Just a short way down the path she caught a glimpse of waves breaking on the shore of a nearby ocean. Another ten feet and she was shading her eyes from the glare of the sun on the sandy desert floor. It was as if every place in the world had been compressed into a few miles, each giving way to the next with the abruptness of the ground meeting the sky in a child's drawing.

The settlements they encountered were just as varied as the landscapes. They passed a town with a space station at its center that Grimsley informed her was a hub for intergalactic travelers. Next, they passed an army of dwarves guarding a fortress built into the mountainside. They smelled like dirty socks and ice cream dishes that had been left under the bed for too long.

As they walked, Grimsley patiently answered Annie's questions. Yes, there were mermaids here. Dragons, fairies, and castles too. There was supposed to be a small colony of dinosaurs, but they kept to themselves in the southernmost region, so he hadn't actually seen them. Of course, Bibylonia had a ruler - Queen Merriweather had ascended to the throne two years ago when her parents had stepped down to take on a second career as alligator wranglers.

"There isn't a king, too?" Annie asked.

"Queen Merriweather is only fourteen years old," Grimsley explained, "and not at all interested in marriage. She has said that she does not wish to have one more person telling her what to do, since her parents spend so much time doing so, and what is the point of being Queen if you can't be in charge?"

Annie thought the queen sounded like her kind of girl.

Watching Marty extend his neck to nip at the arrows on Grimsley's back, something occurred to her.

"Hey, Grimsley," she said, pulling the tiger away by the ruff. "You said you started out as the rabbit from my book. How did you end up like you are now?"

Grimsley adjusted his eyepatch.

"My first memories," he said, "are of a dark, quiet place. Nothing ever changed, until the day I woke to light filtering through a crevice in the rocks. I crept out to get a better look and emerged from a hole in the ground at the edge of a great forest, looking out on a sunny meadow. This was in the earliest days of Bibylonia, and most of the creatures that lived there then walked on four legs, not two.

As time went by," he continued, "the world around us continued to change. The first people arrived, houses were built, then villages, and finally whole cities. Our little meadow grew until it was no longer recognizable as the place where I had been born. I left my warren and went to live in the forest."

"One morning I woke to find a bow and arrows on my back that had not been there when I went to sleep. At the time I had no inkling of how they had come to be there, but I soon encountered other creatures who had acquired such…er…improvements.

We went to speak with the Lady…"

At Annie's questioning look, he elaborated, "The Lady leads the Council of Guardians. She explained to us that the creatures living in the forest are most affected by your imagination because of our proximity to the garden. We are the first to change when you yourself do.

I thank you for the boots, Miss Annie," he added, smiling. "My feet did get cold in the early mornings."

Annie smiled back.

"Okay," she said, "the Council lives in the forest we passed through to get here?"

Grimsley nodded. "We guard the gate, to make sure that no one enters Bibylonia, and that nothing gets out that shouldn't."

Annie wondered briefly why anyone would ever want to leave this place, but before she could ask anything else, she was distracted by the sight of the forest over the rise of the next hill. On the other side, Annie knew, was the gate leading into the garden. Her garden.

A nearby tree rustled as a large black squirrel with a thin, ropy tail scampered quickly through its branches. She was so busy watching the squirrel that she didn't immediately notice the group of people that had emerged from the forest and now stood quietly, awaiting their arrival.

An observer of the previous night's Council meeting would have recognized them as the creatures who had gathered in Annie's dollhouse. They watched in respectful silence as Annie and Grimsley approached, all eyes following their progress.

Grimsley introduced her to each of them, Annie struggling to remember all their names. They escorted Annie to the gate, where she and Marty followed Grimsley back into the garden. Grimsley led her back to the little patch of moss where she had first opened her eyes. Set into the wall behind it was a heavy wooden door she hadn't noticed when she arrived. It was rounded at the top, with no embellishment of any kind, not even a keyhole. One of Grimsley's giant feet left the ground with the effort required to push it open. Beyond it, she saw the familiar shadows of her bedroom, quiet in the semi-darkness of early morning.

"This is your way home, Miss Annie. Simply close the door behind you, and you will wake in your own bed, safe and sound."

"What?" Annie felt panicked. "But I barely got to see anything. Can't we go on a real adventure before I have to go home?"

Grimsley smiled, and there was no trace this time of his usual hesitation or fear. "Don't worry, Miss Annie. Tomorrow night, Bibylonia will be waiting for you."

CHAPTER 9
A RUDE AWAKENING

Annie woke to the insistent blare of her alarm clock. She sat up quickly, hoping to find herself still in the garden. Instead, she was greeted by the bright pink walls of her own bedroom, sunlight streaming through the window.

She had known all along it was just a dream, but she still couldn't control the surge of disappointment she felt. She kicked her feet irritably over the side of the bed and trudged out into the hall. Marty, back in his usual housecat body, wound between her ankles, firmly requesting attention.

Her bad mood lasted through breakfast. After calling Annie's name three times without a response, her mother finally came into the kitchen where she was listlessly spooning cereal into her mouth.

"Annie, what in the world has gotten into you this morning?"

She explained about the dream. Her mother seemed genuinely interested, asking questions about Grimsley and the places she had visited. She laughed out loud at the idea of Marty the tiger.

"I don't know why I'm so disappointed," Annie confessed. "I mean, I knew it was a dream while it was happening. I even tried not to wake up because I didn't want it to end. It just seemed so real."

"You've always had an active imagination," her mother said, resting a hand on top of her head. "When you were little, your dad and I would hear you talking in your room when you were supposed to be taking a nap. You would lie on your back on the floor, telling stories to yourself. The idea of you dreaming up another world seems just right to me."

She leaned over and kissed Annie's cheek before returning to the living room to help Maisy with her shoes.

"Try not to be so sad that it isn't real," she called back over her shoulder, "and try not to miss the bus."

She missed the bus. Her mother almost managed not to sigh when she came back through the front door.

Homeroom was deafeningly loud, as usual. She slid into her seat next to Jay, whose wild, curly hair hung in his face as he hunched over his book. She shook her head, grinning, as she dropped her backpack on the floor between them and fished out her pencil box to double check her homework.

She considered telling him about the dream but found that she wasn't quite ready to share it with anyone else. Maybe she would tell him at recess, when there weren't so many other people around.

When she got to the cafeteria for lunch, Jay was already sitting at a corner table with his lunch spread out in front of him. As usual, he had his nose in a book, his blue eyes darting rapidly across the pages. It was open to an extreme close up of a rattlesnake, its mouth distended around something furry, with the stub of a tail dangling out.

Annie thought of Grimsley and winced.

"Jay, couldn't you find something a little more disgusting to read?" she asked, rolling her eyes as she opened her lunch box. "Looking at that, I hardly want to barf at all."

Jay didn't look up as he pushed his applesauce across the table towards her. She passed her banana into his open hand. Annie's mother was currently on a "no processed foods in the house" kick, so this lunchtime trade was a regular ritual.

Jay's book was pretty interesting once you got past the ick factor. They were so engrossed in it that they didn't notice the new arrivals until their shadows loomed over the table, blocking the light.

They looked up to find Beau and Ashley standing in front of them with identical smirks on their faces.

"Look at that," Ashley said, smiling even more widely. "He never stops studying, even at lunch."

Beau snickered, and Annie felt her face growing hot. She looked quickly over at Jay, but he had already returned to his book.

"Well," Ashley continued, "It's not like he has anything else to do. Like a social life, for instance."

Beau laughed even harder. Annie struggled to come up with something to say – anything - that would shut them up. But her mind was blank; she couldn't think of a single word.

Mercifully, the bell rang, and a cafeteria monitor's voice rang out through the chatter and noise, instructing them to pack up and head for their next class. The twins stepped away from the table and began walking unhurriedly towards the nearest exit, their departure so synchronized that it might have been choreographed.

"Dorks," Annie muttered under her breath as they got up from the table.

"Why can't they just get kicked out of this school already?"

She looked worriedly at Jay, but he appeared to still be completely absorbed in his book, bumping into chairs as he stumbled through the cafeteria. She sighed and grabbed the back of his shirt so she could steer him safely through the crowd.

CHAPTER 10
BACK TO BIBYLONIA

Annie woke the next morning before her alarm clock went off. Even with her eyes closed the room was much too bright. Marty must have pulled the curtains down while she was sleeping again.

She opened her eyes to the sun blazing in the sky above her, and she flung a protective arm in front of her face to shield her eyes from the glare.

She was back in the garden, on the same patch of moss where she had woken before. Marty lay beside her, his tiger's tail twitching in sleep. Delighted, she jumped up and started to look around.

It was the same garden, but then again, it wasn't exactly the same. The winding path was now bordered by rows of tulips in every color of the rainbow. The ivy twisting over the stone walls had sprouted little white flowers, and a patch of neon yellow irises had settled in the middle of the path so that anyone wanting to walk on it would have to step over them. She was pretty sure she could hear them giggling.

Her heart racing, she ran towards the center of the garden, jumping over the irises as she went. She pushed back the sweeping pink branches at the entrance to the clearing so abruptly that a swarm of butterflies erupted from a nearby bush and took to the sky.

He was precisely as she remembered him; nearly her height, with grey fur and long, drooping ears. His bow and arrows lay on the bench behind him. He hadn't yet spotted Annie, standing in the shadows of the trees.

"Hey," she said quietly, trying not to startle him.

She was unsuccessful.

At the sound of her voice, Grimsley leapt straight into the air like a cartoon character. She stumbled backwards in surprise, tripping over a tree root and landing hard on her rear end. She clutched her stomach as she tried

26

valiantly to suppress her laughter.

He hurried forward to help her up, a wide smile on his face. His joyous expression faltered somewhat when he noticed Marty cleaning his paws behind her. Impulsively, she threw her arms around his neck and hugged him.

"I told you I would be waiting for you, Miss Annie," he said, shyly. "Did you bring your key?"

The key. She had woken up in her bedroom after the last dream without it, of course. She put a hopeful hand to her throat, and her fingers closed around the heavy chain.

"Of course I did," she said, grinning. "I think it's time we actually went on an adventure, don't you?"

CHAPTER 11
THE ADVENTURE BEGINS

This time when she entered the forest, she wasn't surprised by the wind that scurried up her legs, or her ensuing transformation. She and Grimsley set off down the path with Marty frolicking behind them, stopping occasionally to chase birds. As they stepped clear of the trees, Annie's breath caught at the sight of Bibylonia stretched out before them, waiting to be explored.

"Um, Grimsley?" she began, having just identified a potential problem. "Usually when the heroes set off, they have, you know, an actual destination in mind. I mean, they're going to save the princess, or the village, or the planet, or whatever. Do we know where we're going?

"I do not," he replied, sounding unconcerned. "But, as you'll recall, this adventuring is as new to me as it is to you. "I expect there are many things you will need to teach me about how it is done, Miss Annie.

"What I do know," he continued, "is that Bibylonia is rarely a quiet place. If we simply remain on the path, something interesting is likely to come our way."

He was quite right. They had only been on the path for a few minutes when they heard a faint sound in the distance. Straining her ears, Annie thought it sounded like someone crying.

"Do you hear that, Grim?" She felt her face stretch into a wide grin. "It sounds like someone needs our help."

In Annie's books, this was when the hero would jump on the back of his trusty horse and ride off to the rescue. She didn't have a horse, but she did have…

Grimsley followed her gaze and took several steps backwards.

"No, Miss Annie. I definitely do not think that's a good idea. I feel certain that whatever the situation is, it can wait…"

His voice trailed off feebly as Annie grabbed a handful of Marty's neck fur and climbed up onto his back. The cat craned his head backwards and dragged his sandpapery tongue across her face.

"Bleagh!" she groaned, wiping slobber off her nose. "Tiger breath. Grimsley, don't be such a baby. He isn't going to hurt you."

Grimsley approached the tiger on trembling legs. When he got close enough, Marty picked him up by the nape of the neck like a kitten and deposited him on his back behind Annie.

In an effort to be understanding, she waited until Grimsley regained consciousness before telling her cat to get moving.

CHAPTER 12
THE TOWER

After a breathless run across the countryside, Annie dug her hands into Marty's neck fur and pulled, the way you would on a horse's reins, and he slowed to a walk. Behind her, Grimsley whimpered quietly.

Just ahead of them was a quaint little village. The streets were lined with tidy shop fronts, each displaying different wares; freshly baked bread with steam rising from its buttery tops, tumbling wedges of wax-covered cheese, stacks of books bound in gleaming leather. Smoke puffed merrily from the chimneys of small stone cottages, their thatched roofs golden in the sunlight.

In the village square a group of children played "Ring Around the Rosie", holding hands and laughing as they fell. Women carrying buckets on long poles over their shoulders passed each other on their way to the well, chattering merrily as they went.

It was the background scenery of every fairy tale she had ever read.

Annie gazed around her at the perfect little town. This was the most amazing dream she had ever had. Everything was just so believable; the colors were bright; the sun was warm on her back and the sound of the children's laughter filled the air around her.

"What is this place?" she called over her shoulder to Grimsley.

"This," Grimsley panted, clinging tightly to Annie's waist, "is the village of Grimm."

Annie thought about that for a moment, then snorted when she made the connection between the idyllic scene and the first compendium of fairy tales she had ever been given. "Of course it is. Cinderella still living at home, or did she eventually make it to that party?"

Grimsley flinched as if he had been poked with something sharp.

"Miss Annie," he whispered urgently into her ear, "that is not something to joke about. Though it has been many years since that dreadful day, the church bells in the village still toll at midnight every night, and they likely always will."

"That dreadful day?" Annie repeated in surprise. "I'm guessing things happened a little differently here than they did in the fairy tale?"

"I would have to assume so," he said anxiously. "In Bibylonia, it is not a story suitable for children."

Curious now, Annie turned her head to ask another question.

"Not now, please." His eyes were pleading. "Ask me again when we are well clear of here, and I will tell you what happened the night the…," Grimsley shivered, "fairy godmother came to town."

They continued down the path until they reached the other side of the village. In the distance stood a forest as vast as the one outside Annie's garden. Between the village and the forest was a rolling green meadow. At its center stood a tall stone tower with a single window at the top.

"Let me guess," Annie said. "This is Rapunzel's place?"

Grimsley shook his head. "She moved several years ago. My understanding is that she found it a bit cramped and went into the city to find an apartment."

"Yeah, I just bet she did," Annie laughed. "So, who lives there now?"

"As far as I know, the tower is deserted. I have heard rumors that the village children dare each other to sneak in from time to time."

"Well, there's someone there now." Annie shaded her eyes with her hand. She could just make out the outline of a figure in the tower window.

"Let's check it out," she said, digging her heels into Marty's sides. Behind her, she heard Grimsley's sharp intake of breath as the tiger's speed increased.

She couldn't help herself. She laughed.

CHAPTER 13
APPEARANCES CAN BE DECEIVING

Annie slid quickly off Marty's back when they reached the tower, craning her neck to get a better look at its occupant. To her surprise, it wasn't the princess she had expected to see, but a boy, maybe a little bit older than she was. A thin silver circlet glinted in his hair. Not a princess then, but a prince.

She called up to him, "Hello! Do you need some help?"

At the sound of her voice, the prince backed away from the window and out of sight.

Confused, she glanced at Grimsley, who looked as puzzled as she felt.

Turning back towards the now empty window, she spotted a black squirrel racing down the side of the tower. She knew she'd seen one like it somewhere recently but couldn't remember exactly where. As she watched, the squirrel reached a small stone ledge set into the base of the tower and sat motionless, like a small, furry gargoyle guarding the...

"Door!" she cried. "Look, Grim, there's a door down at the bottom. That must be how the witch got in before Rapunzel came along."

Looking more closely, she realized why it hadn't been immediately visible. The wood was carefully painted to match the tower stone. It made sense; the witch wouldn't have wanted anyone to see how to get in. In fact, if that squirrel hadn't decided to perch directly above it, she likely wouldn't have spotted it herself.

"Okay," she said, "That's probably how the kids from the village have been getting in and the prince too. So, why is he just sitting up there? Why doesn't he come down the stairs and walk out the door?"

Grimsley didn't respond.

"You know," she said, turning towards him, "I'm not just talking to myself here…"

Her words died in her throat.

Grimsley's arms were still around Marty's neck, as if he had just climbed down. His legs were shaking so badly that one of his hind paws had come free of its boot and was thumping softly on the ground beside it.

Her first thought was that it was just like one of those slow-motion moments in the movies, when the person hasn't realized that the monster is standing right behind them. Even though she knew this was only a dream, an icicle of fear slid down her spine. She turned her head to follow Grimsley's gaze. What she saw when she did made her completely forget that this was "only a dream."

A dragon was emerging from the forest behind the tower, its scaly hide silver-bright in the sun. When the last few feet of its gleaming tail were clear of the trees, it began to run.

Annie had always thought dragons would be clumsy on the ground, but this one moved with the effortless grace of a desert lizard. Its wings tucked neatly against its back, and its hind legs carried its huge body low to the ground for maximum speed. It would have been beautiful to watch, if it hadn't been heading directly for the spot where they were standing.

Annie knew she had only a matter of minutes before it reached them. She also knew they stood no chance of outrunning it, even on Marty; the dragon was simply too quick.

But she had absolutely no clue what to do. She wasn't a knight in shining armor that could dispatch a dragon with a slash of his sword. She didn't even have a sword. Or a knife, or even a baseball bat. Her own dream or not, she was pretty sure she was about to get eaten.

She looked frantically around for a weapon. Maybe she could use the wide leather belt she wore as a whip to keep the dragon at bay. She unbuckled it quickly, and something hard banged against her leg.

And then she remembered. Her first visit to Bibylonia, and the fleeting thought that she needed to get her hair out of her face. She had discovered exactly what she needed in the little drawstring pouch on her belt.

Never taking her eyes off the approaching dragon, she fumbled for the pouch, loosened the string and slipped her hand inside.

Her fingers closed on something smooth and flat, and she quickly pulled it out.

It was a small red book. The words on the front cover were faded by age, but Annie could still read them clearly.

"English/Dragon Dictionary?"

She looked up and noted with alarm that the dragon was a lot closer than the last time she checked. Frantically, without any sense of what she might be looking for, she started flipping pages in the little book, squinting in the sunlight while she read.

The dragon was almost upon them when she found what she was looking for.

"Flrphc!" she shouted.

The dragon skidded to a stop in front of her. If she hadn't been frightened out of her mind, it would have been comical; its hind legs slid around to the front due to the speed of its deceleration, turning it almost all the way around before it managed to right itself.

After several struggling moments, it positioned its body before her in a crouch, close enough that she could smell the smoke gusting from its nostrils as it exhaled. It didn't move. It didn't attack. It simply waited, like a hawk that has spotted a mouse hiding in the grass.

Annie flipped through several more pages until she found a listing of commonly used phrases, looked the dragon straight in the eye and said, "Grkkkkk. Bllllsshhh tphk Annie. Wll Bllllsshhh?"

The dragon's response was immediate. He sat up on his haunches and released a barrage of syllables that sounded a lot like Marty coughing up a hairball. She had no idea what he was trying to say, but at least he was talking rather than eating her. She held up her hand as if to say "wait," and consulted the book again. Ah, there was the word for "slowly."

"Ylgh."

She could have sworn the dragon smiled, although given the size of his teeth that wasn't actually encouraging. He opened his mouth again, and this time he spoke less quickly, giving her time to hunt through her dictionary.

Working painstakingly through the little book, she interpreted the dragon's words to mean, "Nice to meet you, Annie. My name is Harold."

A dragon named…Harold?

"What do you want?" she asked. At least, she hoped that was what she had asked.

Her luck seemed to be holding, though, as the dragon answered her. She flipped through the pages again to interpret.

"The boy," he had said.

Now they were getting somewhere.

"Why?"

"The boy," the dragon repeated, raking deep furrows in the ground with his talons. She didn't need the dictionary to know he was angry. His nostrils had started smoking again.

Annie stood her ground, even though her legs were shaking. This might be only a dream, but it was her dream, and she was not the kind of person who fed princes to dragons. "No."

He shook his head, so vehemently that a tiny flame escaped his nostril, momentarily setting his ear on fire. He slapped at it frantically with his foreleg.

"Okay, listen up," she said, momentarily forgetting to be afraid. "That kid is scared out of his mind up there. I don't know what you want with him but you...you can't have him. I won't let you."

Her voice faltered, as she realized two things simultaneously; she really didn't have any way to make good on that commitment, and also, she hadn't translated any of that into Dragon.

So, it was to her immense surprise that the dragon's head drooped, and he sank to the ground in front of her, his head resting on his front feet. He looked exactly like her sister when she got caught sneaking into Annie's room.

"Hang on," she said, "did you actually understand me just now?"

He nodded, and spoke again in that harsh, guttural voice, this time in English.

"I took a correspondence course through the mail a few years ago. It seemed like the thing to do, given that the village had grown and was now so close to my forest. I thought that when it came time for me to capture one of the village maidens and roast her for my supper it would be easier to do if I could talk to her."

Revolted, and more than a little afraid, Annie stepped backward until she bumped against Marty's broad rib cage.

"And did that work?" she asked.

The dragon sighed.

"I never even tried," he said sadly. "Never really liked roasted maiden all that much. I'm actually a vegetarian, but I can't let the villagers know that or they'd be all over my forest, making a lot of noise, and waking me up during naptime."

Annie shook her head. This was the strangest dream.

"So," she continued, "You're a...vegetarian dragon, living in the forest outside the village. And, you want to be left alone."

He nodded.

"So, why would you go chasing after a prince? You have to know that means the villagers will come after you."

To Annie's surprise, the dragon put both of his front feet over his face, pressing it into the ground so that his smoking breath caused the grass in front of him to curl and turn black. His massive shoulders began to shake, and silver tears fell from his eyes onto the ground.

Of all the things she thought might happen when she first saw the dragon emerging from the forest, watching him cry was not one of them.

Without really thinking about it, she reached into the pouch at her waist as if it were her own pocket and pulled out a dragon-sized handkerchief. She walked over to Harold and patted his shoulder to get his attention, trying not to think about the fact that his talons were longer than her fingers.

He looked up in astonishment. "Thank you," he said, taking the handkerchief and wiping his red reptilian eyes with it.

"You're welcome," she said, sitting down next to him. "Do you, um, want to talk about it?"

She wasn't sure what else to say. How do you comfort a dragon?

In a voice barely more than a whisper, he whimpered, "You'll all laugh at me."

Annie glanced back at Marty and Grimsley, cowering in terror.

"Harold, I don't think they can even hear you right now. Whatever it is, your secret is safe with me."

The dragon brought the handkerchief to his nose and blew it loudly. It exploded into a thousand fragments of burning ash.

"Oh, dear," he said anxiously, holding out the largest remaining piece. "Sorry about that."

"That's all right. I don't need it back," she said hastily. "Look, I promise not to laugh, okay? Just tell me."

This was delivered with a lot more confidence than she felt, but the more she talked with Harold, the more she felt he wasn't quite the monster she had assumed him to be.

"All right," he sniffled, swinging his neck forward and bringing his enormous head close to Annie's face, "but I don't want the rabbit to hear. I want to whisper it to you."

She eyed Harold's claws nervously, but took a deep breath and leaned towards him, cupping her hand around her ear.

At first, all Annie could think about was how hot the dragon's breath was on the side of her face. But then he started talking, and the longer he talked, the angrier she got. When he finally finished whispering, her face was as red as if he had breathed fire on it instead of just infusing her hair with smoke.

"Harold, you wait right here," she told him sternly. And with that, she marched to the foot of the tower and pushed hard on the door, which was locked. Fortunately, she had now been in Bibylonia long enough to know what to do.

She slipped her fingers into her belt pouch and drew out a rusty old iron key. It was, of course, a perfect fit. She unlocked the door and marched inside.

For several minutes there was no sound from the tower except for the echo of Annie's careful footsteps, as the staircase inside the tower wound perilously up to the tiny room at the very top and had to be climbed slowly.

While the distance from the top of the tower was too great for her friends to hear the precise words Annie used while talking to the prince, it was pretty easy to get the general idea. Marty put his paws over his ears and buried his head in the grass. He was very familiar with that particular tone of voice, having spent his whole life in a house with Annie's mother.

After several minutes, she emerged from the tower. She held nothing in her hands, but the front of her tunic bulged oddly in a way that it hadn't before. She walked quickly towards Harold, who was looking determinedly everywhere except at Annie, twisting his head as he examined his feet, the forest, and the sky.

When she was so close that he could no longer avoid it, the dragon finally looked at her. Upon spotting the lump in her clothing, his eyes snapped upwards to meet hers. She grinned at him.

"Here," she said, withdrawing from her tunic a very worn, obviously well-loved teddy bear. She handed it to Harold, angling her body so that the others couldn't see. "I don't think he'll do it again. Right now, I think he's more afraid of me than he is of you."

The dragon could maintain his façade no longer. He cradled the stuffed animal in his forelegs, wrapping his talons around its little body both possessively and incredibly gently. He sat down on the ground with a thump that shook the earth beneath Annie's feet, and began to sob loudly, without a care for who might be watching. Annie patted his massive shoulder while he wept.

After a few minutes, Harold regained enough control to speak again.

"I…I don't know what to say," he choked. "No human has ever done such a thing for one of my kind."

"Yeah, well," she replied, still furious, "he did it to impress his stupid friends, who told him they thought he was too chicken to sneak into your cave and steal some of your gold. When he got there and there wasn't any, he was so angry that he couldn't prove he'd done it, he took your teddy bear just to be a jerk. When you came after him, he headed for the first place he could think of to hide, figuring you'd never be able to get your head in there. I guess he wasn't counting on me showing up."

Through Annie's righteous indignation, she felt a small swell of pride. She had helped someone. Maybe not the someone she had been expecting, but she had done the right thing, and that was all that mattered.

Harold laid his huge, triangular head at her feet. "I am," he said, in a voice still shaky from crying, "forever in your debt, tiny Annie."

And just like that, Annie experienced for the first time in her life what it felt like to be a hero. She placed her hand gently on Harold's head, because it seemed like the right thing to do. She didn't keep it there for long, however. His head was almost as hot as his breath.

She helped him to his feet. "I think," she said, with a little mischief in her voice, "we'd better make sure he's never tempted to do anything like that again."

The prince had fled the tower and was now running towards the trees as fast as he could go.

"Maybe you should chase him into the forest, just to drive the message home. And you might want to breathe a little fire while you do it."

She hesitated for a moment. "Don't eat him, though."

Harold's lips curled back, displaying rows of gleaming, needle-sharp teeth. He huffed out a gust of smoky air in what was unmistakably a laugh. He sprang forward and took off running across the meadow, sending Marty scurrying to hide in the tall grass, and Grimsley into a dead faint on the ground.

Annie watched him go, right up to the point where his tail whipped around the trees at the edge of the forest, breaking branches as he went. The prince's panicked cries were barely audible over the dragon's deafening roars.

She sat down and laughed until her sides ached and she couldn't catch her breath. She hadn't forgotten the Christmas Eve four years ago when her cousin Robbie had stolen Miss Kitty and hidden her, right before bedtime. Maybe the next time they went to visit her cousins, Harold could come along.

When the dragon's roars finally faded away, Annie stood up, brushing away the cinders from her mutilated handkerchief. She walked back over to Grimsley and Marty.

"Well!" she said, happily. "I think that qualifies as a genuine adventure, don't you?"

Grimsley made a sound like air escaping from a balloon.

On the way back to the garden Annie badgered Grimsley to tell her the story of Cinderella, but he refused, peering anxiously around whenever she brought it up. He tried to distract her by pointing out items of interest along the way, including a herd of winged horses grazing in a nearby field (Annie had to tell Marty sternly that he could not chase them) and a gang of ice giants having a snowball fight at the foot of a craggy mountain.

They decided to have a picnic in the meadow outside the forest before returning to the garden. In her pouch, Annie found enough food for an army. There was even a glass bottle of milk and a tiger-sized saucer for Marty.

Pleasantly sleepy once her stomach was full, Annie rolled onto her back and gazed up at the afternoon sky.

What a great day. It hadn't turned out the way she had expected, but she always liked it when that happened in stories. It just went to show that things aren't always what they seem. Harold was a dragon, but he was really a pretty nice guy. And she might only be an eleven-year-old girl, but here...here she was a hero.

CHAPTER 14
BACK TO REALITY

The following day, Annie woke smiling at the memory of Harold chasing the prince into the forest, breathing fire. Her good mood lasted all through getting ready for school. Annie was normally not a morning person, so this resulted in several exchanges of bewildered looks between her parents.

She made it to the bus with five minutes to spare, probably for the first time since she started kindergarten. She spotted a seat in the middle and slid into it quickly, dropping her backpack onto the narrow bench next to her to save a spot for Jay.

You didn't want to sit too close to the front of the bus, because the driver was prone to bouts of excessive chattiness. If you accidentally caught his eye in the rear-view mirror, you were stuck for the rest of the ride. Nobody wanted to sit all the way at the back where the eighth graders were, either; they were notorious for picking on younger kids. Besides, they smelled weird.

Jay's stop was the next one after hers, and when the bus doors creaked open, he stumbled up the stairs with his nose so deeply buried in his book that only the tops of his eyebrows and his curly blond hair were visible.

He was almost within hailing distance when a small, delicate foot in a pink ankle boot suddenly shot out from one of the seats, and Jay tumbled over it, landing flat on his face in the aisle.

As quickly as it had appeared, the foot was gone. Annie jumped up despite the shouted orders from the driver to sit back down right now and hurried to help Jay gather the scattered contents of his backpack. The bus roared with laughter, and Annie glared around furiously as she stuffed pencils, erasers, and books back into Jay's bag.

Ashley's head appeared over the seat back, a malicious smile on her face. Satisfied with her handiwork, she settled back in her seat, her foot dangling idly over the bench into the aisle. Annie had to fight the urge to pull off the little pink boot and throw it out the window.

Meanwhile, Jay had struggled to his feet, dislodging half the contents of his backpack onto the floor again. After they had picked everything up a second time, Jay slid into the seat next to Annie, seemingly unfazed by what had just happened.

"So," he began excitedly, "my dad brought home this totally awesome book last night about species that only exist in the rainforest. Have you ever heard of poison dart frogs? They have some of the best defenses in the animal kingdom. Even the colors of their skin send a warning to predators that they're not safe to eat."

He grinned happily, as if he had just informed her that today was free cupcake day.

As Annie bent her head over Jay's book, she found herself wishing that he had a few defenses of his own. No matter how oblivious he seemed, he had to be at least a little concerned about the fact that he was apparently the twins' new favorite target.

The rest of the day passed without incident, and after the final bell Annie and Jay parked themselves on the sidewalk to wait for the bus, which was running late, as usual. Beau and Ashley weren't among the kids waiting today. Annie hoped they had gotten in trouble for something and ended up having to stay after school.

On the bus, Annie's thoughts kept returning to Bibylonia, and whether she would find herself there tonight. Part of her really wanted to tell Jay about her adventure. In all the years they had been friends, they had never kept secrets from each other. But she hadn't even told her parents about the second dream. For whatever reason, it felt like something that was meant for her alone.

Even though she wasn't quite ready to share the whole truth, she couldn't focus on anything else. So, before long she found herself recounting the story of her daring teddy bear rescue, not as a dream, but as a story she had read the previous evening. By the time she got to the part where she held out her hand and told the dragon to stop, Jay had put down his homework and was listening intently.

When she had finished, Jay said, "I want to read that when you're done. Who wrote it?"

"Oh," Annie hedged. "I don't actually remember. My mom read it to me, so I never saw the cover."

"What's the book called?" he persisted.

Scrambling for anything that sounded convincing, Annie blurted out, "Grimsley, the Guardian of the Gate."

CHAPTER 15
THE MAP

The next time Annie woke in the garden, she wasn't surprised at all. She rolled onto her side and jostled Marty until he grumbled to his feet.

Grimsley was in the clearing, poring over an enormous piece of paper he had spread out on the ground in front of him. When he heard her footsteps approaching, he looked up and gave her a wide smile.

"I found us a map, Miss Annie," he said happily, pointing at the paper.

She grinned back at him. "Sweet, Grim. Where'd it come from?"

His reaction to this question was unexpected. He looked down at his feet and cleared his throat several times before responding. Finally, he muttered something about "Lady Cottontail" being kind enough to loan it to him. Annie noticed that the tips of his ears had turned bright pink.

Annie crouched down to examine it, shaking her hair around her face so he wouldn't see her laughing.

The map was hand-drawn and looked very old. Unlike most maps she had seen, there were no continents, just a large mass of land dotted with landmarks with names like "The Hidden Forest," "The Stormy Sea," and "The Endless Mountains." What lay beyond the borders was anyone's guess. The map simply faded at the edges like someone had taken an eraser to it.

Scanning for a likely place to start, she quickly determined that anywhere in Bibylonia was a good place for an adventure. As she leaned in for a closer look, she felt something warm on her left leg. She sat up and the heat ebbed away, as if she had stepped back from a blazing fire.

Tentatively, she inched closer to the map, ready to pull back if the paper suddenly caught on fire. She smoothed the surface with her fingers, searching for an area that felt warmer than anywhere else and quickly found it; a tiny spot that glowed, as if someone was holding a candle to the underside of the paper. She leaned forward to get a better look.

"The city of Aesoppla," she read. "You ever heard of it, Grim?"

"Yes, Miss Annie." Grimsley's forehead wrinkled in a frown. "I'm not sure Aesoppla is the best place to start an adventure. Not much happens there that is out of the ordinary."

Annie thought that Grimsley's idea of out of the ordinary and her own were unlikely to be the same. Still...

"What did Lady Cottontail say when she loaned you this map, anyway?" she asked. "Her exact words, if you happen to remember them."

Grimsley's ears grew slightly pink again.

"She said, 'Give this map to Miss Annie, for it shall be a beacon to light her way. Even in the darkest of times, her path will be illuminated.'"

He smiled sheepishly. "That's the way she always talks. She is the poet laureate of Bibylonia."

"A beacon to light her way...," Annie repeated.

She was pretty sure by now that she was dealing with magic. If she was right, then the map grew warm to tell her help was needed somewhere, and the glow pointed her in the right direction.

"Excellent!" she shouted, clapping her hands, causing Grimsley to jump in surprise. "Aesoppla it is. Let's hit the road."

Grimsley opened his mouth to argue, but she held up a hand.

"Trust me," she said. "Or, I suppose I should say, trust Lady Cottontail. Today, Aesoppla is definitely the place to be."

And with that, she marched determinedly towards the gate, drawing the great iron key from beneath her nightgown, Grimsley and Marty at her heels.

CHAPTER 16
TICK TOCK

Annie had noticed that geography in Bibylonia seemed to follow its own set of rules. While the map depicted a world that seemed comparable to her own in size, it never seemed to take very long to get anywhere, no matter what their destination was. It was as if the path they traveled folded like an origami animal, compressing great distances so that Annie could arrive in time to save the day and still wake up in her own bed in the morning. So, even though on the map it looked hundreds of miles away, they reached Aesoppla in about ten minutes.

Annie noticed as they approached that some of the houses at its outskirts were very oddly shaped. The first one they passed was unusually low and narrow, like a brick tunnel barely rising above the surface of the ground. There was a tiny cottage with a thatched roof perched halfway up an oak tree. The next house was large enough to comfortably house several families, but it had huge circular holes in the roof, like someone had taken a giant drill to it.

She had just turned her head to ask Grimsley what sort of people lived here when the answer to her question appeared before them.

Wiping her front paws frantically on the frilly green apron she wore, a river otter darted forward to the center of the path and stopped directly in front of them, standing on her back legs. Marty skidded to a halt, so close to the otter that her whiskers quivered.

"Thank goodness you're here," she exclaimed in a high, anxious voice, reaching up with strong furry arms to pull Annie down from the tiger's back. "I don't know what we would have done if you hadn't...but you did, and that's all there is to it. Please say you'll come. You're the only one who can help us."

Before Annie could open her mouth to say, "help you with what?" the otter threw up her paws in apparent exasperation.

"Listen to me," she cried, "blithering away, and there's no time to waste! Hurry, hurry, we must hurry!"

The otter took Annie's hand and led her towards the city. She moved so quickly; Annie had to jog to keep from being dragged behind her. Their frantic pace didn't stop Annie from staring in amazement at the sight of Aesoppla, however.

As cities went, it wasn't terribly unusual in the way it had been designed. There were sidewalks and streetlamps, apartment buildings and shop fronts, just like you might see in any city anywhere.

What made Aesoppla stare-worthy was the city's inhabitants. Animals. Everywhere she looked there were animals. Like the otter that was guiding her, they were all wearing clothes. Also like the otter, most of them were walking on their back legs like people.

There were two monkeys in business suits reading newspapers on a park bench. Through the window of a corner store she saw a zebra behind the counter, doling out change to a fox wearing a hoodie and baggy blue jeans. There was even an alligator riding a bicycle, although later when Annie tried to explain how this had looked, she was at a loss to find words to describe it.

They stopped before a handsome building constructed from enormous round stones, like river rocks, smooth and gleaming in the afternoon sun. Annie looked back at Grimsley quizzically, who shrugged his shoulders. It seemed he had no clearer idea of what they were doing there than she did.

She followed the otter through the door and down a long narrow hallway lit with old-fashioned oil lamps in brackets on the walls. As she walked, she felt a strange sponginess under her feet, as if the earth was giving way a little with every step she took. She looked down and saw that instead of a solid floor, the ground was covered with a layer of thin, flexible twigs that had been woven together to form a sort of carpet. She had never seen anything like it before, but it was surprisingly pleasant to walk on.

When they reached the end of the hall, the otter opened yet another door into a small bedroom with wood-paneled walls. In the center of this room was a sturdy little bed, just big enough for a child. It appeared to have been built from solid tree trunks; bark still covered the wood in places. Another oil lamp sat upon the bedside table, casting its glow on the creature that lay sleeping there.

Having never seen one in the wild, Annie nevertheless knew immediately that the animal was a beaver. He wore a long nightshirt patterned with red and white stripes and a matching nightcap. The blankets were neatly tucked around his waist, the outline of his wide flat tail just visible beneath them and his tiny paws folded across his chest. An ornately carved wooden cane was hooked around the bedpost by his head.

It was like something out of one of the illustrated fairy tale books her grandmother used to read to her. Well, she thought, given the circumstances, it probably was something out of one of those books.

They were not the only ones in the room. There were animals standing at every window and on either side of the door, quite obviously guards. All their eyes were trained on the bed and its inhabitant.

The otter moved to the beaver's bedside, where she briskly straightened his nightcap and laid her paw against his forehead. Then she turned to face Annie and spoke for the first time since taking her hand on the path.

"He is our clock-keeper," she said. "And he will not wake."

Annie was getting used to that moment that came after someone had explained something in a way they thought was perfectly clear, but she still had no idea what was going on. It seemed to be a regular occurrence in Bibylonia. So, instead of asking what a clock-keeper was, she waited. As she gazed on the peaceful face of the sleeping animal, she heard Grimsley clear his throat behind her.

"Miss Annie, the clock-keeper of Aesoppla is probably the most important resident of the city. It is a title passed down from mother or father to son or daughter. The clock-keeper is responsible for the creation of new clocks, and for the repair of existing ones. Without him, the city could lose track of time."

The guards shifted uncomfortably at these words, and the otter's paws twitched.

"Okay," Annie said slowly, "Obviously there's something I'm not getting here. I mean, I like to know what time it is too, but we're not talking about the world coming to an end, right?"

She was completely unprepared for the reaction she got to this question. Everyone began talking at once, several of the guards burst into tears; one frantic raccoon actually fell to the ground with his tiny paws over his eyes. Only the otter remained calm, moving through the room and speaking quietly to each of the animals in turn.

After the noise had subsided, she returned to Annie, taking her hands and leading her to two high-backed chairs underneath a small circular window, where they sat down. The chairs were obviously designed for creatures with shorter legs than Annie's; she felt like an adult at a child's tea party.

"I'm afraid the end of the world is exactly what we're talking about," the otter said, sadly. "At least, for our city and our way of life. "

For the next twenty minutes, the little otter, who Annie had begun referring to as Mrs. Otter in her head, described a civilization that was completely governed by…time. Everything about their society operated on a schedule so strict that it would make an army general green with envy. The bell tower in the center of town chimed at five-minute intervals, all day and all night. Everyone in town rose for the day at precisely six. The children arrived at school not one minute past eight. Shops opened for business at nine on the nose. Lunchtime for everyone, from babies to businessmen, was at noon. Every moment of their lives was accounted for. No one was ever late. No one was ever early. It sounded like her mother's idea of heaven.

Annie also thought it sounded terribly boring. What if your game of tag was more exciting than usual, and you had to stop playing because play time was over? Or if you had been given green beans for supper, which were so disgusting that you had to swallow them whole and wash them down with milk? That took a lot of time, and if you didn't finish, you wouldn't be getting dessert. And how on earth could anyone sleep with that bell ringing every five minutes all night? She supposed they were just used to it since it had always been that way.

She had a thought. "You said taking care of the clock is something that gets passed down to the clock-keeper's kids, right? Can't one of them do it until he wakes up?"

The otter sighed. "Our clock-keeper is very young. He has no children to assume this responsibility for him."

"Oh," she said, feeling deflated. "So, what happens if the bell tower breaks, and the clock-keeper isn't there to fix it?"

Mrs. Otter shuddered. In a voice that could barely be heard, she whispered, "We will not know when to eat, so we will not eat. We will not know when to go to work, or to school, so the shops will not open, and the children will not learn. We will not know when to sleep, so we will stay awake until our bodies shut down from exhaustion. Then, without the clock, we will not know when to wake again. We have always had the clock to guide us. Without it, we lose track of not just time, but our lives."

Horrified, Annie stood up and went to the beaver's bedside, shaking him gently by the shoulders. No response. She shook him again, a little more roughly this time. Still nothing. She leaned over so that her mouth was directly by his ear, and said loudly, "Wake up!"

The beaver slept on.

"How long has he been like this?" she asked.

"Three weeks," said the otter. "We despaired of ever waking him until we heard of your arrival in Bibylonia. You must find the antidote to the sleeping potion he has been given."

Of course. Now it made sense that he wasn't waking up even with someone shouting in his ear.

"Do you know where the sleeping potion came from?"

More muttering broke out among the animals. It sounded angry this time.

Mrs. Otter raised one paw and spoke sternly, "Quiet. They cannot help being what they are."

Annie was reminded of her mother and how she always tried to rationalize to Annie why her little sister was such a brat.

"Who can't help being what they are?" Annie asked.

"None but the wood elves of the Evergreen Forest would have had reason, or opportunity to do such a thing," Mrs. Otter said, "We found the clock-keeper sleeping in the grass beside the well after he failed to return home for the noon-time meal, and the well is close enough to the forest to throw stones at."

"In fact," she said ruefully, "it's not unusual for the elves to throw stones at visitors to the well from their hiding place in the trees. They are mischievous creatures, and I'm sure they would have found the idea of interrupting our schedules quite entertaining. However, I do not believe," and here she cast a forbidding glance around the room, "that they realized how much damage could be done by what I'm sure they only perceived as an excellent joke."

"This forest, can you tell me how to get there?"

The otter shook her head. "The forest would be impossible to travel for any who had not spent hours on its paths. You must have a guide, or you will never reach the wood elves' camp. I will send our most experienced navigator with you."

The otter stepped back into the hallway and opened another door that led into a small courtyard behind the house.

"There's no time to lose. The clock has never gone so long without maintenance before."

She clapped her paws, and something rose slowly from the tall grass. It was huge, at least fifteen feet long, its graceful body as flexible as a rope. As it turned its round, glassy eyes towards them, she saw that its neck was strangely curved, like the bowl of a spoon. No one who had been friends with Jay Lucas for the last five years could have failed to recognize this creature. A king cobra.

CHAPTER 17
THE GUIDE

Annie stumbled over the threshold in her desperation to get back into the house. She grabbed Mrs. Otter by the paw and pulled at her insistently, never taking her eyes off the snake racing towards them.

The otter looked up at Annie's terrified face.

"My dear, whatever is wrong?" she asked, clearly concerned.

Annie lifted a badly shaking hand to point at the approaching predator.

"Don't worry," Mrs. Otter said reassuringly, "you could have no better guide than Clarence. He knows the way, and he can travel as quickly as your tiger can. He is your best hope for finding the antidote in time."

At the sound of his name, the cobra had stopped in his...track, just feet away from the open door.

"Aw, shucks," he said, in a soft Southern drawl, "I reckon the little lady's afraid I'll take a bite outta her."

Annie dropped Mrs. Otter's paw in shock, her other hand still on the doorknob. For a moment she had forgotten where she was; a land where dragons slept with teddy bears and the fairy godmother was an urban legend. She had only seen a predator moving towards her and never thought for a moment that he might be the guide she had been promised.

The snake dipped his hooded head in her direction. "Mighty pleased to meetcha, Miss Annie."

She couldn't understand why he didn't lisp with fangs that huge.

"Um. Nice to meet you too, Clarence." Annie was glad that her voice only trembled a little. "So, you're my guide, then?"

"Yes'm," he said, cheerfully. "Don't suppose there's anybody in Aesoppla that knows that forest better'n I do."

"Well, then." Even though her voice now sounded almost normal, she had to hold on to the doorframe to support her trembling legs as she turned towards the house. "Let me just get the others and we'll be on our way."

Marty flatly refused to come into the yard with Clarence. One look at the snake and he fled back inside to hide under the beaver's tiny bed, most of his body sticking out from underneath it. Annie had to get help from the guards to drag him out so that they could set off.

Riding towards the forest, Annie found Grimsley's quiet whimpering against her back almost reassuring. At least she wasn't the only one who was uneasy about setting off through the forest with one of the deadliest creatures in the world. Marty seemed to be coping fairly well after his initial breakdown, although whenever Clarence turned his head towards them, the big cat made a gagging sound, like he had a hairball caught in his throat.

If his traveling companions were unnerved by his presence, the very sociable cobra seemed completely oblivious to it. He chattered away merrily as he guided them through the trees, telling them all about his childhood, growing up in Aesoppla. The shapes of those houses made a lot more sense to Annie now that she had met some of the city's inhabitants.

He had twenty-five brothers and sisters, most still living at home with their parents. He was the city's lone police officer, but there wasn't really any crime to speak of in Aesoppla. So, he spent most of his days wandering the forests that surrounded the city.

"An' that's how come I got to be in charge of this here expedition," he explained. "I reckon I've spent more time in these woods than I have in town."

Because Clarence seemed to be in a sharing sort of mood (and because it was the first time he had stopped talking long enough for her to get a word in edgewise), Annie posed the question she had been dying to ask since the first time he opened his mouth.

"Hey, Clarence, you said you were born and raised in Aesoppla."

He nodded happily.

"So, how come you sound like my Aunt Rachel from Arkansas?"

Clarence chuckled.

"Well, y'see," he said, "with so many of us to mind, Ma kept pretty busy. We got some scheduled free time in the mornings after the older kids headed off for school, and Ma really needed that hour to keep up with things. So, as soon as we were old enough to hold our hoods up, we got parked in front of the television for a spell.

We don't get a lot of call for TV here," he continued. "Some o' them stations show more commercials than actual shows nowadays. When that happens, sometimes things go a bit over their time. Well, you can't have folks running late first thing. So, the local station puts on a couple of old-timey shows in the morning instead. Fewer commercial breaks make it easier to stay on schedule."

"Don't tell me," said Annie, grinning. "One of those 'old-timey shows' was The Beverly Hillbillies?"

Her grandparents watched reruns of that show. Black and white, with a prerecorded laugh track and bad jokes told in worse Southern accents, Annie had never understood why they thought it was funny.

"Yes'm," he confirmed. "And Hee-Haw. That one was always my favorite. 'Cause of the music, you see. I just love it when they have that Johnny Cash on. He sure does sing some fine tunes. Do you like Johnny Cash?"

Since she had no idea who Johnny Cash was, Annie asked another question instead of answering him.

"So, why doesn't everyone in Aesoppla talk like you? If you all grew up watching these shows and that's how you learned how to talk, I mean."

Clarence looked perplexed, and Annie had the insane thought that he would be scratching his head if he only had arms.

"Can't rightly say why that'd be, Miss Annie. Like I said, we watched TV every morning so Ma could get things done. Don't know that I recall any of our friends mentioning that they did the same. Could be that most folks found something else to do with that time."

She turned her head quickly so he wouldn't see her smiling. It wasn't that she was afraid. At this point she had lost all fear of Clarence, just as she had with Harold the dragon. She just didn't want him to think she was making fun of him. After all, cobras had feelings too.

"Tell me about the wood elves," she asked. "What are they like?"

Clarence's round eyes narrowed, and his hood flared slightly.

"They're hooligans, that's what they are. We don't allow them into the city, but they're always wanderin' around the edge of the forest, causin' as much trouble as they can. Throwin' snowballs when it snows, and spitballs when it don't. They've even been known to tie shoelaces together while folks are visitin' the well or rig the buckets so they dump water on your head when they come up to the top."

"Hmm," Annie said, thoughtfully. His description reminded her of someone. She remembered coming home the previous year in tears because of a classmate's constant practical jokes – pulling her chair out from underneath her when she sat down and knocking over her books. Her mother had gently explained that some kids tease not to be mean, but because they just don't know how to have a conversation with you. It had helped Annie to understand that Michael probably didn't realize he was hurting her feelings. After a few weeks of sitting at the same table, Annie got used to his teasing, and eventually she even came to consider him a friend.

"They sound a lot like a kid I know," she said. "He takes things too far sometimes, but he's not a bad person. I have to agree with Mrs. Otter. I think maybe they just didn't realize the trouble they would cause."

She was still thinking this over when Clarence stopped abruptly, directly in front of them. She tumbled off Marty's back in a crackle of fallen leaves, and the cobra whipped his head around. Before Annie could even sit up, his hooded face was inches from hers, eyes blinking rapidly. For a brief moment her terror was back; all she could see when she looked at him was her own ugly death, but then he spoke softly, "Shhhh, Miss Annie. We need to be right quiet now. We're almost there."

He extended the end of his long tail, and she used it to pull herself up from the ground. As she stood, she spotted a flickering light through the dense trees a few yards ahead of them. The growth pattern of those trees didn't seem natural to Annie. They formed a nearly perfect inward curve, with branches that sprouted low on their trunks, intertwining to form a nearly impenetrable wall of leaves. Another one of those black squirrels was swinging from the branches like a trapeze artist.

They crept forward, Clarence gliding noiselessly across the ground. The rest of them made soft crunching sounds when they moved. Annie was sure the elves would hear them coming, but she needn't have worried. As they grew closer, it became obvious that the amount of noise the elves themselves were making was more than sufficient to cover their approach.

Annie tiptoed towards the place where she had seen light through the trees. She noticed a bare spot in the greenery at about waist height, and grabbing a nearby tree branch for balance, she leaned forward and peered through.

What she saw in the elves' encampment looked a lot like her school's playground at recess; there were paper airplanes sailing through the air, people running in every direction, and a great deal of shouting and general clowning around. The only unusual thing was the size of the people. From what she could see, the tallest of the elves would only come up to Annie's knees.

They were dressed in what she thought of as "Robin Hood clothes," leather tunics over leggings in the colors of the forest floor. Annie didn't even see one prankster hiding in the bushes until his victim tripped over an invisible string that hoisted him into the air to dangle in the trees.

She gestured to Clarence to take her place at the peephole. He slithered forward and pressed his face against the gap in the trees. Almost immediately, he pulled away and turned back to Annie, eyes wide with horror. Annie stifled a laugh. To someone who had lived his whole life in orderly Aesoppla, the scene would be like something out of a nightmare.

Suddenly, a shoe sailed through the air above them, coming to rest in the leaves a few feet away. A small, darting figure emerged from the enclosure, parting the tangle of branches as if they were water. With his attention so focused on the shoe he was chasing, the elf didn't realize he wasn't alone until he tripped over a coil of Clarence's tail and fell, landing hard at their feet.

Laughing, he rolled over onto his back, but his amusement died at the sight of a giant, a tiger, and an enormous snake. He opened and closed his mouth several times like a fish, then collapsed bonelessly onto the ground in a dead faint.

CHAPTER 18
BOYS WILL BE BOYS

"Well," said Clarence, with satisfaction, "that was easier' n shootin' fish in a barrel." He tilted his head slightly. "Can't say that I ever understood that sayin', though. I mean, why would you put fish in a barrel in the first place?"

Annie looked down at the unconscious face of the wood elf they had accidentally captured. He looked young, maybe about her age. A green skull cap fit snugly around his head, with only a few carrot-colored curls escaping. His angular face was generously spattered with freckles.

The elf began to stir, stretching his legs like a cat waking up from a nap. When he tried to raise his arms over his head, he encountered resistance in the form of a length of rope Grimsley had taken from his boot. Finding himself bound, he suddenly became quite still. After a moment he opened bright blue eyes and looked appraisingly at Annie.

Now that they actually had an elf at their mercy, Annie wasn't sure what to do next. There hadn't been time to make a plan – he had simply fallen into their laps like a gift. She had a feeling that interrogating him wouldn't get them what they needed, so she sat down cross-legged in the leaves facing him and waited.

They stared at each other for a long time. Just when she felt like her face would explode if she didn't say something, the elf broke the silence.

His voice was surprisingly deep, especially coming from a person that small.

"So," he said, "you came. They said you would, but I never believed them."

Annie blinked. Was there anyone in this place who didn't know who she was?

"Of course I came," she said, trying to sound stern. "Do you have any idea what you've done?"

He smirked. "Sure, I do. Put the old rat to sleep, didn't we? You should've seen his face when the spell hit him. Tipped over like a pot of molasses!"

Even though every instinct she had told her to stay calm, Annie felt her cheeks grow hot. She wanted to take the elf by the shoulders and shake him until he told them where the antidote was.

Instead, she said, as reasonably as she could manage, "The city needs their clock-keeper. No one else knows how to do what he does."

The elf looked at her shrewdly. "Still sleeping, then, is he? Wonder how long before the clock breaks down and the rest of them end up running around like chickens with their heads cut off?"

He slapped his knees with his still-bound hands, rocking back and forth as he shook with laughter.

Annie's patience evaporated.

"It's not funny!" she snapped at him furiously.

That only made him laugh harder.

Annie stood up quickly and strode away towards the trees, afraid that otherwise she would end up punching the obnoxious little jerk. Grimsley came to stand beside her.

"Pardon, Miss Annie," he said timidly, "but perhaps it is time to see what help your pouch has to offer."

She had completely forgotten. Quickly, she untied the drawstring that held the pouch closed and pulled out...a jar of peanut butter, a small carton of milk, and an enormous spoon.

Annie stared at this odd assortment of items, wishing that her little bag of tricks came with an instruction manual. She wasn't about to sit down and have a snack with the elf. She couldn't even have a conversation with him, for pity's sake.

She had tried reasoning with him, and he had reacted...well...like a ten-year-old boy. She looked down at the objects in her hands and wondered; what would her prankster friend Michael do with the objects she held in her hands?

It took her a surprisingly short period of time to come up with an answer. She tucked the milk back into her pouch and walked towards the smirking elf on the ground. Thinking about what she planned to do, it was easy enough to put an answering smile on her own face.

"Grim, I need you to hold his mouth open for me. Clarence," she continued, when the elf gave Grimsley a mutinous look, "If he struggles, bite him."

Clarence narrowed his eyes menacingly, which was probably overkill given the fact that he was a giant cobra.

Even though she knew he wasn't as terrifying as he looked, she still felt the need to whisper, "I'm bluffing, by the way. Definitely don't bite him," as she walked past.

The elf was convinced. He held perfectly still and allowed Grimsley to pry open his jaws. Annie knelt in front of him, holding her spoon like a weapon. Never taking her eyes off the elf's face, she dipped the spoon into the jar of peanut butter and scooped out a large dollop. She ladled it into his open mouth.

The elf's reaction was almost comical. His eyes widened in surprise, and his tongue slid out to lick the corners of his mouth. Apparently peanut butter was new to Bibylonia. When she put the spoon back into the jar to dig out some more, however, he frowned. She could almost hear him thinking, "There's not enough room in my mouth for another bite."

Wrong. She pushed the second spoonful into his still-open mouth, and then another, and another, until his cheeks were as wide as a chipmunk's. She stepped back to admire her handiwork.

"You can let go now, Grim," she said, stifling a giggle at the beginnings of panic on the elf's formerly cocky face. She watched him work his jaws back and forth, trying to dislodge the peanut butter so that he could begin to swallow it. The longer he tried, the more anxious he became. When his efforts became so frantic that she worried he would faint again, she delivered her final blow.

"There's no point, you know," she said confidently. "Your mouth will be stuck like that forever unless I give you the antidote."

The elf stopped pushing at his face with his fingers and looked at her warily.

"There's a price," she continued. "Before you get your antidote, you have to give me the clock-keeper's. As soon as I have it in my hand, I'll cure you."

Almost before she had finished speaking, the elf was on his feet. He ran through the trees and disappeared into the encampment.

Annie glanced over at Grimsley, who shrugged. Clarence looked confused as well, but it's not easy for a snake to shrug, so he shook his head instead.

The elf re-emerged as quickly as he had disappeared. He skidded to a stop in front of Annie, holding out his still-bound hands. She found it hard to look at his bulging cheeks without laughing. She opened her hands beneath his, and something small, smooth, and shiny dropped into them.

A coffee bean.

"What do I have to do?" she asked. "Make him swallow it?"

The elf shook his head and mimed putting something in his mouth and closing it.

"So I just have to get it into his mouth?"

The elf nodded vigorously.

Annie felt a giant grin break over her face. They had done it! She tucked the coffee bean carefully into her belt pouch and pulled out the carton of milk and a straw that had materialized next to it. The elf was already reaching out for them when she had a sudden thought. She pulled them back out of his reach.

"This better not be another prank," she said sharply. "If this doesn't work, I'll send Clarence back into the woods after you. He's the best tracker there is, and he'll have no problem finding you. Right, Clarence?"

The cobra rose to his full height. He leaned over until his hood was mere inches from the top of the elf's head and made a loud sniffing noise. "Got his scent now, Miss Annie. Could find him in a barn full o' foxes if I had to."

The elf shuddered, but didn't take his eyes from Annie's

Annie untied the rope around his wrists and handed him the milk. He moaned with relief as the liquid slowly began to dissolve the sticky mess that had immobilized his jaws.

When he was able to speak again, he said, with wonder in his voice, "What was that stuff, lady?"

She laughed. "It's called peanut butter, and it's actually pretty tasty when you don't have an entire mouth full of it."

"And the antidote?" he asked.

"Milk is what I gave you, but any liquid would work. You just needed something to loosen it up. Eventually your spit would have done it, but that would have taken a really long time. And also, that's really gross."

He stared at her. "So, you mean to tell me that if I had just bided my time, I wouldn't have needed your help? I gave up the rat's cure for nothing?"

"Pretty much," she said cheerfully, tightening the thongs on her little pouch.

She was prepared for the elf to get angry. After all, she had tricked him, and then played on his panic to get what she needed. She was not, however, prepared for him to burst out laughing.

The elf bent over with his hands on his knees, howling until he gasped for air. When he had finally regained his composure, he stepped forward, holding out his hand to her. He wore a broad grin on his face, as if they were meeting for the first time instead of concluding a hostage situation.

"The name's Will Sykes, Miss Annie. Knew who you were the minute I saw you, of course."

She took his tiny hand, oddly strong in her own.

"They," Annie took this to mean the other elves, "told me you'd come to try to save the rat, but they never told me you were so wily."

He looked at her curiously. "Are you sure there's not elf in your family tree somewhere?"

She had tied him up, threatened his life, and tricked him into giving up his people's secret and he was…impressed?

"I don't think so," she said, "I'm not exactly from around here."

He shook his head, still smiling. "No, I suppose not. That was a great trick, though. You wouldn't be willing to leave the rest of that with me, would you?" he said, gesturing at the peanut butter with a sly look. "Seeing as how you're about to shut down our best prank in years, it'd be nice to have something to bring back to the boys in exchange."

She handed over the peanut butter jar and spoon, feeling that the elves were less likely to do significant damage with peanut butter than with sleeping potions. Hopefully, anyway.

The elf swept off his little cap and sank into a deep bow. "Until next time, Miss Annie," he said, his eyes bright with mischief.

She watched him scamper back to the trees and disappear into the hidden encampment. She almost felt sorry for the other elves. She had a feeling Will would want to try out his new toy right away.

CHAPTER 19
RISE AND SHINE

The return journey to Aesoppla seemed much shorter than their trek into the forest. This was twice that Annie had been presented with what appeared to be an impossible task, only to succeed in saving the day. She couldn't stop smiling, even when Marty stopped to hack up a poodle-sized hairball.

As they walked, Clarence talked ceaselessly and animatedly of life in Aesoppla.

"So, Clarence," Annie asked with genuine curiosity, "What do you do when you're not helping capture elves? Do you have any hobbies?"

She imagined the giant snake manipulating a pair of knitting needles with his tail and had to stifle a laugh.

"Yes'm, I surely do," he said happily. "Whenever we have scheduled free time, I like to play a game of chess with my best friend Bob. He's the best player in Aesoppla, 'cept me, of course."

He smiled modestly.

The idea of Clarence playing chess was almost as strange as the vision she'd had of him knitting. "That sounds…nice," she said. "Have you been friends a long time?"

"Since I was a hatchling and he was a pup!" he replied. "We were born on the very same day."

"Oh," said Annie, surprised. "Is Bob a dog?"

Clarence let out a hearty guffaw. "Nah, he's a mongoose. Looks more like a weasel than a dog. Pretty funny lookin' critter, to tell you the truth, but he's good company."

Annie waited for Clarence to tell her he was joking, but he continued to chatter on about the last time he had defeated Bob at chess.

Not every kid Annie's age would know that the mongoose is famous for its ability to kill venomous snakes, but because of Jay's reptile obsession, Annie had seen quite a few YouTube videos on the subject. She tried to imagine the two animals sitting down with a pot of tea and a chessboard instead, without much success.

The scene at the little house was exactly as they had left it. Annie walked quickly across the bedroom floor and gently pried the beaver's jaws open with the fingers of one hand, dropping the coffee bean onto his tongue with the other. His paws began to twitch the moment the coffee bean touched his tongue, causing the otter to leap to her feet, dropping her teacup to the floor.

The beaver sat up abruptly, as if waking from a quick catnap instead of a two-week coma. He reached over and unhooked his cane from the bedpost before hopping down to waddle towards the closet. After retrieving a pair of overalls and brown work boots, he looked pointedly around at the other animals, who immediately rushed for the door, back into their everyday lives.

Mrs. Otter and Clarence walked with them to the edge of town. The otter bestowed a whiskery kiss on Annie's cheek before quickly scurrying away. Annie guessed that after three weeks of watching over the beaver she was desperate to return to her usual routine.

They said goodbye to Clarence next, promising to return to watch him compete in the annual All-Aesoppla Chess Tournament.

She and Grimsley climbed on Marty's back and headed towards the garden. She glanced back when she heard the big village clock chiming brightly and smiled. It sounded like they had made it in time.

Turning back to the path, she caught movement out of the corner of her eye. When she looked around for the source there was no one there, just rolling green hills and a wide, empty plain in the distance. Even so, she had the strangest feeling that they were being watched.

CHAPTER 20
AN ORDINARY DAY

Weekends were the only time no one in the Albright household had to get up early. So, when Annie woke on Saturday morning, she pulled the blankets over her head, hoping to fall asleep again and find herself back in Bibylonia.

It was no use. The sun was high in the sky, and Marty had progressed beyond his usual gentle scratching at her door to a rhythmic beating that sounded a lot like someone playing the drums. She opened it and picked him up. Together they wandered down the stairs in search of breakfast.

The rest of her family was on the sofa watching a movie. "Your breakfast is on the kitchen counter," her mother told her, glancing up from the screen.

She grabbed her plate and plopped down next to her dad. The movie was one of her favorites, but for whatever reason she wasn't really in the mood for TV. So, when she finished eating, she headed back up to her room to look for something to do.

On her desk she found the book she had been reading the night she first woke up in Bibylonia. Smiling at the memory, she picked it up and stretched out in a patch of sunlight on her bedroom floor. Unfortunately, this story also failed to capture her attention. After reading the same page three times, she put the book down, quickly got dressed and headed to the garage to get her bike.

The day was sunny and unseasonably warm for October. When she got to the cul-de-sac, she found most of the neighborhood engaged in a water balloon fight. She parked her bike at the curb and ran over to join her friends Katie and Zoey, who were hiding behind the big magnolia tree in Katie's front yard with a bucket of ammunition. Annie managed to shut down one of the other teams (once you were hit, you were out) without ever getting hit herself, but after about fifteen minutes she lost interest in this too. She said goodbye to her friends and climbed back on her bike to head home.

Annie couldn't understand what was wrong with her. It was a perfect day; no school, no obligations. It would normally have stretched delightfully out in front of her with endless opportunities for fun. If only Grimsley and Marty had been here to share it with her, but Marty was an indoor cat in this world, and Grimsley…well, Grimsley wasn't real.

The problem, she thought, was that her perspective had changed since her introduction to Bibylonia. There was just no comparison to the possibilities that presented themselves when she opened her eyes in that other place, even if it was only a dream.

She coasted down the road into her driveway. After parking her bike by the garage door, she trudged over to her father, who was scooping leaves into a plastic bag, and sat down in the middle of the pile he was working on. He made a mock grumpy face as he continued to clear the leaves around her.

"What's up?" he asked. "Nobody home this morning?"

"Yeah, they're all out in the cul-de-sac, throwing water balloons," she replied morosely. "I didn't feel like doing that today."

Her father's eyebrows went up under the tops of his wire-framed glasses. Annie shrugged. "I guess I'm just bored."

He stood up, leaning on the handle of the garden rake as he looked at her. Finally, after several minutes during which she didn't quite meet his gaze, he said, "Well, when your sister gets up from her nap, we're going to the science museum. Why don't you get yourself a snack, and change clothes so you'll be ready?"

Annie perked up a little at this news. The museum was always worth a trip. Divided into different sections for the various branches of science, there were live animals, fossils, even a lab where you could participate in experiments along with the museum employees. It was one of Annie's favorite places in the world. Well, in this world, anyway. She hurried up the stairs to find some dry clothes.

At the museum, they visited all her usual haunts - the archaeological "dig" where you got to keep whatever bits of fossilized shell and rock you could find, the rescue center where the veterinarians cared for animals that had been injured in the wild, and her favorite, the oceanography exhibit with the giant submarine-shaped playground at its center.

Frequently the museum housed temporary exhibits in addition to the permanent fixtures. Today's guest star was a huge display from a deep-sea exploration that had yielded up the centuries-missing treasure of the legendary pirate James Downing, who had been born right here in Annie's hometown.

She had learned about him the previous year when they had to research an historical figure for school. He had been the son of a prominent businessman until he grew bored following in his father's footsteps and abandoned his home to join a band of pirates. After twenty years of stealing from any ship that ventured too close to his own, he had disappeared, never to be heard from again.

Annie wandered around the exhibit, examining the pieces of history that had been rescued from the ocean floor: a pile of gemstones cloudy with age, a battered gold necklace long enough that she could have worn it as a belt, a scattering of tarnished coins.

She tried to imagine what it would have been like for Downing to live as a pirate after having grown up as a normal kid. Did he miss his family? What about other things that most people take for granted but that would be luxuries at sea, like fresh fruit or a soft bed? What would she miss if she woke up one morning to find she was still in Bibylonia, never to return home? Her mom and dad, of course. Jay, absolutely. Her sister…well, that would kind of depend on how much of a jerk she was being that day. Other than that? She really wasn't sure anymore.

CHAPTER 21
A TOWN IS BORN

Annie opened her eyes to sunlight in the garden, triumphant at having yet again managed to dream herself back to Bibylonia. She stood up, nudging a sleeping Marty with her toes, and began to look around for Grimsley.

Immediately she noticed how much the garden had grown since her last visit. The flowers were now so tall that she couldn't see over them, and the gate was completely covered with ivy. The place had a feeling of untended wildness about it, like the yard of an abandoned house.

As she stood surveying these changes, Grimsley emerged from the clearing. He hurried down the overgrown path to meet her. To Annie's surprise, after greeting her he reached out and stroked the fur between Marty's ears. She noticed that he was trembling slightly as he did this, but she was still impressed.

"Hey, Grim," she asked curiously, "What's up with the garden today?"

Grimsley looked surprised. Apparently, he hadn't noticed anything unusual.

"Just as the creatures that live in the forest change with you, Miss Annie, so does the garden. As such, it is never quite the same two days in a row."

Annie supposed that made sense. And she understood why the flowers had suddenly grown so wild – her discovery of Bibylonia had her imagination in overdrive.

Grimsley extracted the map Lady Cottontail had given him from his boot and spread it out on the garden path. Annie crouched down, looking for any indication of where their help might be needed. Unlike last time, however, the map stayed stubbornly cool, with no sign of hot spots anywhere. She rocked back onto her heels and looked at Grimsley, who seemed as perplexed as she was.

"I don't get it," she said. "Last time we could tell right away where we were supposed to go. Do you think it's broken?"

Grimsley gazed at the map. "I don't think so, Miss Annie," he said slowly. "I think it's possible that at this very moment, there is no one in Bibylonia in need of a hero."

Annie's shoulders slumped. She had been waiting all day to get here, and now that she was here, there was nothing to do?

The way she was feeling must have shown on her face, as Grimsley hastily continued.

"However, that is certain to change. Perhaps we could take this opportunity to explore? There are many places in Bibylonia you haven't yet seen."

Annie still felt disappointed but didn't want to say no to the hopeful look on Grimsley's face. She opened the gate, careful as always to lock it behind them. After the usual transformation into her Bibylonia self, they set off down the path.

Annie held the map out in front of her as they walked, scanning for a likely destination, and trusting Grimsley to warn her if she was about to tumble over a cliff. As she was inspecting an amusement park with the intriguing name "Edible Adventures," she suddenly spotted movement towards the bottom of the map. She stopped walking and laid it out on the ground to get a better look, hoping for that spark of warmth and light that would tell her they had someplace to be.

Instead, she was amazed to see drawings appear on the paper. They were faint at first, but took shape quickly, like a charcoal rubbing of a gravestone. Buildings that hadn't been there before blossomed into being before her eyes, along with a delicately scripted legend that gave the name of the new settlement.

"Downingsburg," she read in disbelief.

The town was shaped like a "U." She traced its curved outline, and the delicately rendered waves that showed it had been built around...

"A harbor," Grimsley said, looking over her shoulder. "A big one, too. I wonder why they chose to build that way, with every property bordering the water?"

Annie was pretty sure she knew why. "Because the founder of the town is a pirate. He wants to be able to reach the ocean from wherever he is."

Grimsley blinked at her.

"Oh," Annie said. "I figured it out from the name. Downing is a famous pirate in my world, so I just assumed...hey, wait a minute."

It had just occurred to her that since this was her dream, she had literally brought this little town to life. Even though she knew that she had imagined everything she'd seen in Bibylonia, watching it happen on the map made it seem more real, somehow.

"Grim, how does this work?" she asked eagerly. "I mean, I'm pretty sure this town just showed up because of what I was thinking about today before I got here. Can I change things whenever I want to?"

Grimsley shook his head. "I do not think so, Miss Annie. Not yet, anyway. The Lady says that you will eventually gain that level of control, but it will take concentrated study."

That was a disappointment. The idea of choosing her own adventure each night certainly had appeal. Then again, one of the things she liked about Bibylonia was that nothing was ever quite what you expected.

Grimsley pointed at a small cluster of caves located a short distance out to sea. "There is trouble brewing there, Miss Annie."

"Why?" she asked, pressing her own fingers to the paper. It was cool to the touch, no tell-tale heat or glowing light.

"Mermaids," he said simply.

Annie looked more closely at the drawing. Sure enough, there was a wide, flat tail poking out of the water beside one of the caves.

"Why does that mean trouble?"

Grimsley shook his head dismally. "Mermaids and pirates are like oil and water," he said. "They don't mix. For a pirate to have built a town so close to their caves, well, it won't be long before there's a full-blown war going on."

"Well," she said, climbing onto Marty's back, "sounds like we might have a chance to get there before the trouble starts this time."

Grimsley climbed up behind her, looking resigned.

"Yes, Miss Annie," he sighed. "That's what I thought you'd say."

CHAPTER 22
THE BATTLE FOR DOWNINGSBURG

The pirate town was exactly how she would have imagined it (she had to remind herself that she did imagine it). The streets were lined with rows of nearly identical saloons, noisy and raucous, with music spilling out of the doorways that Annie was pretty sure her parents would not be comfortable with her hearing. There were munitions shops here and there as well, with neat rows of cannon balls lining the window fronts like giant black marbles.

The houses appeared to be cobbled together from the remnants of old ships, with portholes for windows and telescopes mounted on the fence posts. There was even a wooden maiden in the center of a ragtag little garden, an enormous birds' nest perched on her wild mane of black hair.

At the center of town was a dock, just wide enough for the ship that was anchored there. The ship was obviously very old, with tattered sails and bolts lined with rust. Algae coated its sides a good five feet above the water line. It had once been painted red, and the bright paint still showed through in places beneath the barnacles. Faded lettering in darker paint was barely visible on the stern, but too little of it had survived the test of time to be legible. Unless, of course, you already knew what it said.

"The Wayward Lad," she whispered. She had known from the moment she had seen it that it could be none other than James Downing's ship. And did her eyes deceive her, or was that Downing himself striding across the deck? She had only seen paintings at the museum, but it certainly looked like him; tall and thin, with wild, tangled red hair down to his shoulders.

She turned wondering eyes to Grimsley, who had climbed off Marty's back and was holding up his arms to help her down.

"Grim, that can't be...I mean, it isn't the real James Downing, right?

Nobody knows what happened to him, but he must have died hundreds of years ago. And anyway, I thought you said nothing from my world could get into Bibylonia other than me and Marty?"

"No, Miss Annie." Grimsley shook his head. "The garden simply used the image you held of this pirate in your mind." He paused, looking slightly troubled. "Although, it is not true that nothing else could cross between our two worlds. That is why the gate must be kept locked at all times."

Annie looked at him, surprised, but before she could ask what he meant, a giant wall of water rose up at the edge of the dock, knocking the pirates off their feet with its force. The barrels they had been carrying tumbled into the ocean as the enormous wave raced towards the center of town like a raging river.

She jumped on Marty's back, pulling Grimsley quickly on behind her as they tried to outrun the water. They did, but just barely, watching from the safety of the street as the last of it lapped gently against the cobblestones. Marty chuffed unhappily. Even as a tiger, that cat did not like getting wet.

Annie spotted a flash of color in the water at the end of the dock. She ran towards it, Grimsley protesting feebly behind her. Mermaids. At least forty or fifty of them. One of them hissed at her, slapping at the water with the end of her tail. Now she understood what had happened. The mermaids had used their collective strength to push the water over the pirates like a blanket.

Annie was still trying to decide whether to speak to them when a cannonball soared overhead, missing her by inches. It landed between two of the mermaids with a loud splash, and they shook their fists angrily at the pirate ship as they began to churn the water with their tails again. It occurred to Annie that she didn't actually know what would happen in the real world if she got hurt in Bibylonia, so she hastily returned to the street to watch from a safer distance.

From there, they watched the battle unfold, Annie monitoring for any sign that one group or the other needed her help. Grimsley inspected the map periodically to see if the town had become a "hot spot." But the map stayed cool, and after a while Annie noticed something unusual. Sure, the pirates were tossing cannonballs off the sides of the ship every few minutes, but somehow, they never seemed to hit any of the mermaids. And the mermaids, who were pitching water onto the dock until not a single board was left dry, always seemed to wait to launch their next volley until the pirates had gotten back on their feet. It looked a lot more like one of her neighborhood water balloon fights than an actual war.

She laughed suddenly, causing Grimsley to jump.

"Grim," she said, delightedly, "this isn't a war, it's a game."

Grimsley looked dubious, but Annie was sure she was right. Certain enough to join in? And if so, on which side?

She walked carefully back down the slippery dock. She approached the edge and looked down at the mermaids in the water. They were now hurling live crabs onto the boards, which scuttled madly around, nipping at the pirates' ankles. She looked up at the ship and saw that someone was looking back at her.

James Downing stood at the prow of The Wayward Lad, watching her try to decide what to do next. He smiled, and for a moment she saw not the fearsome pirate he had become, but the restless boy he had been. He unhooked a heavy rope from a gleaming brass hook and lowered it down to her. She climbed onto the knot at the end and held on tight as he pulled her slowly up the side of the ship.

When she reached the top, he helped her onto the deck, and she could finally see the full picture of the battle. Dozens of pirates ran in frantic circles around the dock, trying to dislodge crabs from the toes of their boots or the seats of their pants. Some had fallen in and were battling mermaids in the water with short wooden swords like those she remembered from Peter Pan. The dinghies hanging off the sides of the ship had been flooded, and the ship itself was so waterlogged that it wouldn't dry out even if the sun shone for a week straight.

She looked up at the pirate captain, who was surveying the scene with great amusement.

"I think you're losing," she said, wryly.

He laughed, a great booming sound. "Aye, that we are, lass. I'll have to give up my hat by nightfall, for certain." He didn't sound terribly concerned.

They were still watching when the mermaids dragged the last pirate into the water and began to tie their captives together with rope from their own ship.

She turned to Downing. "Your men made it really easy for the mermaids to take them down. I think you could have won that fight," she said. "Why didn't you?"

He chuckled. "It's time I had somewhere to call my own, Miss Annie. This is a quiet enough place to settle down, and I can still smell the sea when I wake in the mornings. If the price for that is losing a skirmish or two, I'm willing to pay it."

She noticed for the first time that his red hair was streaked with grey, and there were deep lines around his mouth and eyes. At the museum she had wondered what he might have missed about his old life. From the way it sounded, the thing he had missed the most about his home was…home.

"And now," he said, "your chariot awaits, my lady."

He gestured grandly at the dock, and she looked down to see Grimsley, already on Marty's back, looking up at her.

She smiled up at him. "I hope you like it here, Mr. Downing."

He returned her smile. "I'm sure I will. And I thank you for the care you took with it." He extended the rope again, and she grabbed hold with both hands. He lowered her gently to the dock as if she weighed no more than a feather, tipped his hat, and vanished from sight.

Annie was quiet on the way back to the garden, still thinking about Downing. Something about her interaction with him troubled her, but she couldn't put her finger on what it was. Maybe it was that she couldn't imagine making his choice, to settle down and leave a life of adventure behind. Still, his face had been so peaceful as he talked about staying in the little town for the rest of his days. Whether or not it made sense to her, she was glad to be responsible for it.

Not quite ready to return home, Annie convinced Grimsley to stop and inspect the map for other places to visit. Being an eleven-year-old girl, she had a natural candidate in mind.

Edible Adventures lived up to Annie's expectations and then some. Everything in the enormous amusement park was made of candy. The Ferris wheel spokes were peppermint sticks, the swings dangled on thick ropes of red licorice. Even the ride tickets were sheets of candy buttons, a different color for each.

Just before the exit there was a magnificent merry-go-round bearing the words "Candy Carousel" across its green and white striped top. Instead of brightly painted ponies there were life-size animal crackers, painted with glossy frosting and mounted on enormous lollipop sticks. A group of monkeys in top hats was already seated, waiting for the ride to begin.

She tried very hard to walk, not run, towards the animal she had chosen, a magnificent circus lion with lemon drops for eyes. She climbed on and motioned to Grimsley to join her. He shook his head, looking faintly nauseated. With a shudder, the ride started up. Marty whined, and swiped his giant paw in the carousel's direction.

Her lion rose and fell gently. She watched the landscape of Bibylonia slowly cycle past. At that moment, she felt like she could stay right where she was forever.

The ride was over far too quickly, and Annie reluctantly climbed down. Grimsley was pulling hard at Marty's ruff to keep the tiger from advancing on the merry-go-round. There were deep furrows in the ground where Marty had dragged him five or six feet forward in his attempt to get to Annie.

She rumpled her cat's ears affectionately. "Don't worry," she reassured him, "I'm not looking to replace you. I don't think I'd get very far on his back."

Annie wrapped one arm around Marty's neck, and tucked the other through Grimsley's elbow. Together, they walked through the exit and back onto the path towards home.

The gates closed automatically behind them, so they never looked back at the merry-go-round, which sat idle, waiting for new riders. They didn't see the ride operator step from his little hut to stand beside one of the carousel mounts, a gleaming white horse with a silver-dusted horn. As the man watched them go, he put his hand on the animal's back. There was a funny crunching sound as it pulled loose from its lollipop stick and stepped off the platform on legs that were suddenly long and grey and skeletal, and no longer sweet at all.

CHAPTER 23
THE SNEAK ATTACK

Annie woke on Monday with a sense of disappointment that had become all too familiar over the past few weeks. It was hard to be an ordinary sixth grader by day and a hero by night.

Annie usually looked forward to school, but right now it was just one more thing she had to sit through until she could be where she wanted to be.

Her mood improved somewhat at recess, though. It was another warm day, and it's hard to be grumpy when you're soaring through the air on a swing in the sunshine. She, Jay, and Mary Rigsby were having an enthusiastic discussion about their shared dislike of the music teacher, which was probably why none of them noticed when two people quietly approached them from behind.

Annie saw Jay fly out of his swing, and for a moment he seemed to be falling in slow motion. By the time he hit the ground, Beau and Ashley were already walking nonchalantly away towards the basketball court.

Annie jumped out of her swing when she was still really too high to do so, feeling the jolt of the hard ground as she landed. Ignoring the sting in her heels, she hurried over to Jay. For several minutes all he could do was try to get enough air in his lungs. Just when Annie was starting to think she had better go get some help, he took in a deep, shuddering breath and let it out again.

"My mom is going to kill me," he said, mournfully.

He held out the front of his shirt, streaked with vibrant green from where he had skidded across the ground.

"Come on," Annie said, helping him up. "Ms. Ward keeps a stain stick in the guidance office. I'm pretty sure if we explain you're going to get killed she'll let us borrow it."

Annie kept an arm around Jay's waist as they walked - he was still a little unsteady on his feet. He stumbled on the uneven sidewalk, and Annie bent forward quickly to catch him before he fell. As he straightened up, she saw that there were tears streaming silently down his face.

In all the years they had been friends, she had never seen Jay cry.

Desperate for some way to distract him from his misery, Annie began telling him about her previous night's adventure. Like before, she made it sound like it was part of a book she was reading. It seemed like an appropriate story to tell, as she had been dealing with some ice giants who had played a prank on the children from the Village of Everlasting Snow.

The children had come out of their schoolhouse at recess for their usual snowball fight with the giants, but over the course of the game they had all gotten tired and collapsed in the snow to rest. While they lay there, one of the giants had the idea to tell the children that their feet tasted like popsicles. Of course, they had believed it, and within moments every child in the village had his or her tongue stuck fast to the toes of an ice giant.

The giants had laughed uproariously, telling them that they would have to stay until first thaw and keep them company, and Annie had found them all struggling in a panic to get free. In her pouch she had discovered a thermos of hot chocolate. There was no question in Annie's mind this time about what she was supposed to do. She tipped some of the warm drink into the open mouth of the nearest child. Not only did it immediately free his tongue, it also melted a significant portion of the ice giant's ankle as it dribbled down the boy's chin, making the giant howl with pain.

Holding up the thermos, Annie had promised the others the same treatment unless they immediately released their captives. There was a blast of steam so intense it fogged the air around them. When it cleared the children were free and clamoring to Annie for their own taste of hot chocolate. Annie had made all the ice giants apologize and promise to play more nicely in the future.

"You see, Jay?" she said, reassuringly. "Bullies get what's coming to them in the end. You just have to stand up to them."

He smiled weakly. "Not sure how I'm supposed to do that when I can barely stand. Anyway, I'm not good at that kind of stuff. They'll find somebody else to pick on soon. I just need to stay out of their way until they do."

The idea of Jay trying to hide from the twins for the next month until they chose another target made Annie sick to her stomach. Feeling frustrated and helpless, she tightened her arm protectively around her friend, and they walked the rest of the way to the guidance office in silence.

CHAPTER 24
A PLAN GOES AWRY

After her mother closed the door to her room at bedtime that night, Annie lay awake in the dark for a long time, the memory of Jay's silent tears still weighing on her mind. There had to be something she could do, but what? Confronting the twins wasn't likely to do any good. If anything, it might just make them pick on Jay more.

Annie sat up abruptly. She had suddenly remembered that there was someone who specialized in dealing with situations like this, someone who already knew that something had happened on the playground the day before. With an actual plan to do something germinating in her brain, Annie was finally able to settle down to sleep.

The following morning Annie's alarm went off half an hour earlier than usual. She dressed quickly and hurried down the stairs to the kitchen, where her father was eating oatmeal while he skimmed the morning news on his laptop.

"Hey, kiddo," he looked up, surprised. "What are you doing up already?"

"I totally forgot that I'm supposed to be working on a project at school," she said, feigning anxiousness.

While the sixth graders were indeed sorting Thanksgiving donations for the local homeless shelter, Annie had no intention of doing any work on this until later that afternoon when the rest of her class would also be taking part. The not-quite-truth made her a little uneasy. She didn't often lie to her parents.

Her dad smiled. "So, I'm guessing you need to get there a little early today?" he asked.

She nodded.

"You're in luck. It just so happens that I'm heading over to your school in a few minutes. I have to switch out some desktops in the computer lab this morning."

Annie knew this already, having overheard her parents talking about it the previous evening. The awareness that she had a way to get to school forty-five minutes early was the seed from which her plan had sprouted.

"So," she asked, innocently, "I can catch a ride with you?"

"Sure," he said. "But I'm leaving in five minutes, so if you're not ready by then, it's the bus for you."

Annie's father chatted happily in the car about the new computers he was setting up that morning, a donation from a local real estate agency. He didn't notice that Annie was preoccupied, which probably wasn't too surprising. Annie had never been much of a morning person. At school, they parted ways near the gym, her dad heading down the north hallway towards the computer lab. Once he had turned the corner, Annie took off for the guidance office, where she and Jay had gone the previous afternoon in search of help with his grass-stained shirt.

The door was open. The guidance counselor was sitting at her desk, poring over a stack of papers with one pen tucked behind her ear and another in her hand.

Ms. Ward was new, having taken over when Mr. Nash retired the previous year. She was young, with brown hair in a messy ponytail, and wire-framed glasses that were constantly slipping down her nose. There was something friendly about her face, something that made you think she'd be easy to talk to. Annie was about to find out.

She stepped through the door, making a little more noise than was strictly necessary. No reaction. Annie cleared her throat. Still nothing. Annie smiled. Ms. Ward was notorious for being oblivious to what was going on around her.

Annie walked over to the desk and put her bookbag down on it. Ms. Ward jumped and dropped both of her pens.

"Annie!" she cried. "Where did you come from?"

"Hi, Ms. Ward," she said. "I was hoping I could talk to you for a few minutes."

The guidance counselor smiled up at her. "What can I do for you today? Another playground mishap?"

Annie looked back at the open door for a moment, then remembered that it was only seven-fifteen. The other kids wouldn't arrive for almost an hour.

"Actually," she said, sitting down, "it's kind of still about the first one."

She started by explaining about the twins' attack on Jay on the playground, but pretty soon she found herself telling her about all the other problems he'd had with them, too, like the incident on the school bus a few days before, and their constant harassment in class.

"This is serious stuff," Ms. Ward frowned. "Why didn't Jay say anything when you were here yesterday?"

"He doesn't think it'll help," she said. "He thinks they'll leave him alone if he ignores it long enough, but he shouldn't have to do that. Everybody knows they're bullies, and nobody does anything about it."

"Annie, did anyone actually see Beau or Ashley push Jay off his swing?"

Annie started to say, "Of course, I was right there," but then she realized that she hadn't seen it happen. In fact, she didn't even know which of them had done it.

"I'm sorry," Ms. Ward said gently, "but unfortunately that doesn't leave us with a whole lot of options."

Annie opened her mouth to protest, but Ms. Ward continued.

"I agree it's unlikely that Jay should come out of the swing so abruptly without someone pushing him, and that the twins' presence behind him right afterwards is pretty suspicious. But, unless someone saw them actually push him, it's your word against theirs."

Annie had known this would be her answer from the moment she had asked about witnesses, but it didn't make it any easier to hear.

Ms. Ward seemed to know how she was feeling. "What I can do is arrange a supervised meeting between Jay, Beau and Ashley to talk out their differences. But to even do that, I would need Jay to come to me himself."

Annie tried to imagine how a meeting like that would go. Jay would sit silently, hoping it would all go away, while the twins faked confusion, very convincingly, about what they were doing there in the first place. And after it was over…they would come down harder on Jay than ever before.

"I don't see that doing a whole lot of good," Annie said glumly. "But, thanks. I know you'd help if you could." She reached for her backpack, intending to head to her classroom and read until school started.

Ms. Ward reached across the desk and covered Annie's hand with her own. The unexpected kindness did what talking about Jay's situation hadn't; Annie's eyes filled with tears. She blinked furiously to keep them at bay. She hated crying. It made her feel so helpless, and she was already feeling helpless enough.

Looking away from the guidance counselor's sympathetic face towards the window that faced the main hallway, she spotted one of the few things that could make this moment worse; her dad, coming directly their way. She pulled her hand free and began wiping frantically at her eyes with the bottom of her shirt.

Ms. Ward followed Annie's gaze to the hallway, then looked back at Annie's panicked expression. As if he could sense their eyes on him, her dad turned in their direction.

"Here," whispered Ms. Ward, shoving a sheaf of papers from the top of the pile on her desk into Annie's hands.

Confused, Annie looked down and saw a poorly drawn turkey on the top sheet, with a checklist of items for the Thanksgiving food drive that she had provided as the pretense for coming to school early. She looked up in amazement. Was the guidance counselor seriously about to cover for her with her own father?

Annie's father appeared in the open doorway, a puzzled look on his face. "What are you doing down here, kiddo? I thought you were going to be working in your classroom this morning?"

Annie held up the stack of papers with the checklist clearly emblazoned on the front page and gave her father the most convincing smile she could muster.

"Thanks for taking those, Annie," Ms. Ward said warmly. "You know I hate leaving my desk. After all, this is where all the excitement is."

Her father's face cleared immediately.

"Speaking of which, Colleen, are you aware that you already have two miscreants out in the hall, awaiting your judgment?"

He grinned broadly. "Not sure how they've managed to get in trouble when the school day hasn't even started yet. They must be overachievers."

Ms. Ward raised her eyebrows. She got up and walked around her desk to peer out into the hallway at the long wooden bench outside the door. She pulled her head back abruptly, her expression horrified.

Her father laughed at the look on her face.

"Must be repeat offenders," he said. "Boy, I'm not sure I'd want your job. At least when a computer misbehaves you can turn it off."

He kissed Annie's check before heading back down the hallway towards the main entrance.

"You'd better get to class, Annie," Ms. Ward said quietly. "We'll talk more later."

Annie was pretty sure who she would find sitting on the bench as she moved slowly towards the door. Ms. Ward's face had given it away. And from the looks on the twins' faces as she walked past them, they had heard every word she said.

CHAPTER 25
DISTRACTED AND DISTRAUGHT

Annie spent the rest of the day checking behind her wherever she went. She knew there would be consequences for telling a teacher and waiting around to see what those would be was making her a little crazy.

After leaving Ms. Ward's office, she had trudged down to her classroom and collapsed into her chair, laying her head down on the desk.

She didn't remember closing her eyes, but she must have because she woke to the shrill sound of the homeroom bell overhead. She sat up quickly, her head spinning.

Jay slid into his seat in a flurry of loose paper and falling books as usual. He grinned at her as he bent down to pick up his homework folder from the floor.

She wanted to tell him what had happened before the twins arrived, but when he straightened up, she saw the spreading bruise that had blossomed on his cheekbone overnight, a souvenir of his fall on the playground the day before. Suddenly she couldn't bring herself to say a word.

Even without looking towards the door, Annie knew when Beau and Ashley arrived, right at the final bell, as usual. Ashley's heels made a distinctive clicking sound as she crossed the room to her customary seat by the window.

Mr. Walliford cast a stern look in their direction before returning to the problems he was copying onto the white board. Annie kept her eyes resolutely forward. Even though she couldn't see them, she imagined she could feel them watching her.

On the playground at recess, Jay started towards the climbing structure. One of their favorite games was to hang upside down from its bars and let the blood rush to their heads while they talked. But the climbing structure was at the very edge of the playground, far away from where the recess monitors stood to keep watch. After what had happened to Jay on the playground the day before, she wanted to be near witnesses right now.

"I think I'd better not climb today," she told him. "My stomach is feeling kind of weird."

"Okay, what do you want to do instead?" His face suddenly brightened. "I have a new book about parasites that I checked out from the library over the weekend. We could look at that!"

Annie thought that after a few minutes with that book her stomach really would be upset, but she didn't want to hurt Jay's feelings. Besides, sitting on one of the benches with a book would keep them in plain view of everyone, exactly where she wanted to be.

"Yeah, go grab it," she said, trying to sound more enthusiastic than she felt.

He disappeared through the doors into the school. Annie sat down, scanning the playground for any sign of the twins. She spotted them, perched on the top row of the bleachers like a pair of vultures.

As she watched, Beau's head swiveled in her direction. He jabbed Ashley in the side with his elbow and she turned towards Annie as well. Annie looked quickly away.

At lunch Annie managed to find a table near the cashier, and she and Jay stayed there until the twins left the cafeteria. When the bell rang at the end of the day, she quickly gathered Jay's things up as well as her own. They were out the door and into the teeming hallway before the twins could get out of their seats.

Out in the courtyard, Annie was feeling pretty pleased about the way she had orchestrated things. She knew she wouldn't be able to arrange every day so that the twins could never get near her, but maybe she could manage it until this blew over? She turned towards Jay and smiled, her first genuine smile since that morning.

He smiled back, completely unaware that his own day had been just as carefully coordinated as hers.

"Is your dad picking you up today," he asked, "or are you riding the bus?"

And just like that, all of Annie's plans fell apart. The bus. How could she have forgotten about the bus? There would be no way to avoid the twins there.

She looked around, hoping against hope that this would be one of those days that the twins ended up in detention, but she was out of luck. There they were, standing at the front of the bus line with a group of kids from Annie's class that functioned as their entourage, following them around and laughing at their jokes.

Annie had read the expression "her heart sank" a hundred times in books but had never really understood what it meant until now. It felt like hers had taken up residence in her left shoe. Her face felt too hot, her hands too cold, and her blood was pumping like she had just run a race.

When the bus arrived a few minutes later, Jay was telling her all about the crawdads he had caught in a mason jar from the creek in his backyard. He seemed oblivious to the fact that Annie hadn't responded to him at all.

Just this once, Annie would have preferred to sit closer to the front, but those seats were all taken before they got aboard. They had to walk past the twins to get to the first empty row. Annie averted her eyes as they went past, but at the last moment her gaze slid over to them involuntarily. Beau was speaking quietly into his sister's ear, but Ashley's round blue eyes were fixed on Annie, and she was smiling. This was not reassuring at all.

Annie slid across the seat, tossing her backpack onto the floor and slouching down as far as she could go. She had never actually played dodgeball; their PE teacher called it "barbaric," but she had seen other kids playing it at recess. She suspected that the defensive team felt a lot like she did right now, like she was in the middle of the longest flinch in the world.

Jay had climbed onto the seat next to her, dropping his pencil case and his science book on the floor in the process. She couldn't believe it. He was still talking.

"…so I told my mom, 'It's the perfect pet. We don't even have to buy food because I can get dead fish out of the creek for them to eat.' She wasn't crazy about the idea of keeping minnows in the refrigerator, though. She says I have to take them back out tonight and dump them." He sighed dejectedly as he leaned over to retrieve his fallen belongings.

When he straightened back up, holding his science book, and Annie still hadn't spoken, it finally occurred to Jay that something might be wrong. He peered at her curiously through his hair, which flopped over his eyes like a sheepdog's fur.

"What's up with you?" he asked.

"Nothing," she said tensely. But the words felt wrong even as they came out of her mouth. He was her best friend; they had always told each other everything.

But before she could tell Jay what had happened, Ashley's voice rang out through the bus as if it was amplified.

"Oh, Andy," she called. "Your friend Jane has lost her pencils. Can you come get them for her?"

This made so little sense that Annie forgot to be anxious for a moment and sat up to see what was going on. Ashley was looking straight at her. Protruding from her dainty fist was a handful of pencils. Pencils decorated with the skeletal outlines of various dinosaur species. Unmistakably Jay's.

Ashley's smile widened.

"Whoops," she said, "my bad. I got confused about who was who for a minute."

She looked pointedly at Jay's too-long hair, then at Annie's faded blue jeans and Adventure Time t-shirt.

"I'm sure that happens to you all the time."

Annie's face flushed with humiliation as she realized what Ashley was hinting at. Most of the girls at her school were seriously into clothes. Some of them were even starting to wear makeup to school. She just didn't see the point. She wasn't really interested in boys, and wearing dresses made it impossible to do anything fun at recess. But she definitely still looked like a girl. And Jay didn't look like a girl at all. Okay, his hair was a little long, and his cheeks were always pink, but that was because he held his face in his hands when he was reading.

True or not, Ashley's dig seemed to have hit its mark. The bus exploded with laughter, drowning out the driver's shouts for them to quiet down. The twins had settled back into their seats, but the damage was done. Annie knew that by the time she and Jay arrived in homeroom tomorrow morning, every single kid in the school would have heard about it. They would be Andy and Jane for the rest of the year. And there wouldn't be a thing they could do to stop it.

CHAPTER 26
NEITHER HERE NOR THERE

Unfortunately, Annie had been quite right. Their new nicknames were all over the school by the following day, along with the knowledge that she and Jay were the twins' current favorite targets. She had never been one of the cliquey kids, but she had always gotten along pretty well with most people. Now she found, to her dismay, that kids she had always liked, even considered friends, gave her a wide berth whenever Beau and Ashley were around. She didn't blame them; she could understand being willing to do anything to stay off their radar, but that didn't make it hurt any less.

Most of the next few weeks passed in a state of nervous anticipation as she tried to prepare herself for whatever might be coming next. In fact, even when nothing did happen, it didn't relieve her stress at all. It was almost better when they tipped their trash onto her lunch table as they passed or aimed the kickball at her head in PE. At least then she wasn't waiting for it anymore.

Her only source of comfort was Jay. Being together didn't really afford them any protection against the twins, but it did make their bullying more bearable. She had the feeling it was the same for him, but neither of them ever discussed what was happening; it was as if talking about it would only make it more real.

Instead, they talked about Bibylonia. Each day at lunch and on the playground, Annie filled his ears with "stories" about mermaids, dragons, and most of all, Grimsley. Talking about Grimsley made her feel a little braver somehow. At least she wasn't afraid of everything.

At home, she went through the motions of doing homework and eating supper with her family, but she grew increasingly restless as the evening hours passed, waiting for it to be time to sleep.

If she hadn't been so preoccupied, she would have noticed her parents exchanging concerned looks while she picked at her food every night. She hadn't told them about the situation with the twins. Her mother would be at the school in a heartbeat, demanding to speak with the principal if she found out, and Annie had already gotten a taste of how much good it did to tell somebody about the bullying. If the twins found out she had told her parents, too…well, she might as well start bugging them now to move to a different school district. Possibly a different state. Maybe she could go to school in Bibylonia, and then she wouldn't ever have to face the twins again.

CHAPTER 27
TROUBLE IN PARADISE

Annie only really felt happy now in Bibylonia. At least in her dreams she was still a hero, not someone who was constantly looking over her shoulder or staring straight ahead in class, trying to pretend she couldn't hear the whispers and laughter behind her. In Bibylonia, she was still in control.

Until suddenly, she wasn't.

The adventure began like any other. She opened her eyes in the garden, woke Marty, and went to find Grimsley. He looked up, smiling as she pushed the branches at the entrance aside. As usual, he already had the map in front of him. She smiled back and felt some of the tension of the day ebb away at the sight of her friend.

"Hey, Grim," she said. "Any hot spots yet?"

"Indeed, Miss Annie," he said happily. Annie crouched down to check out their destination.

It appeared to be one of the many meadows in Bibylonia. There were scattered outlines of flowers and short, thin brushstrokes here and there that suggested grass. In the center was a circle of words, written in the same delicate cursive as everything else on the map, repeating over and over until the loop was closed.

"World's beginning, world's end," Annie read, tilting her head to follow the sloping script. "What does that mean? How can it be both the beginning and the end?"

"It is my home," said Grimsley, and his voice quivered with excitement. It was so different from his usual tone that Annie lifted her head from the map to stare at him.

"This is the meadow you told me about? The one you found when you came out to see where the sunlight was coming from?"

"Yes, Miss Annie," he nodded. "It was the site of the world's beginning, for all life in Bibylonia originated there. And it was also the end, when the meadow changed so much that it was no longer the world itself, but a memory of what had been."

Grimsley smoothed the edges of the map, a reverent expression on his face.

"It is perhaps the most sacred place in all of Bibylonia," he went on. "To visit the meadow without cause is not permitted, but the map is clearly telling us that those who still live there are in need of assistance."

The meadow. It was where Grimsley had come from, where all of it had come from. Suddenly, she couldn't wait to see it.

"Come on, buddy," she said, pulling him to his feet. "Let's go."

The meadow was on the other side of Bibylonia, but as usual, it took only a few minutes to get there. On the way, Grimsley talked incessantly about his home.

"Of course, it's much smaller than it used to be," he told her excitedly. "When I first left my warren, the meadow stretched out in every direction as far as the eye could see. That was before you learned to read, Miss Annie. Then everything changed. I think the Endless Mountains appeared the week you turned seven."

He smiled at the memory. "That was a real surprise, the morning we woke to find mountains where there had been none the night before."

Just then a small white mouse darted onto the path in front of them, stopping to gape in horror at Marty. It was dressed as somberly as a funeral director, in a black suit with a tiny cane in its paw. As Annie watched, the mouse shot off the path like a rocket into a nearby bush. She glanced over her shoulder, curious to see what the mouse was running from, and spotted a man standing between two trees at the edge of a distant forest.

"Hey, Grimsley, who is that?" she asked.

Grimsley followed her gaze. "Where, Miss Annie?"

She frowned at him. It was hard to see clearly because the sun was so bright, but she didn't see how you could miss that there was someone there. When she looked back, however, the man was nowhere to be seen. Maybe she had imagined it, because she had been looking for whatever was chasing the mouse.

As they crested the top of the next hill, the meadow lay below them like a vast rolling carpet, lush and impossibly green. Tall grasses drifted lazily in the afternoon breeze, sprinkled with delicate wildflowers that looked like they would blow away if the wind got too strong. It was beautiful, but in a completely different way than her garden was beautiful. While her garden was wildly alive, the meadow seemed like a sleeping place, tranquil and still.

She slid off Marty's back and reached up to help Grimsley down, but one look at his face told her that something was very wrong.

"What is it?" she asked, worriedly.

Grimsley walked slowly down the hill and sat down in the tall grass. Annie followed, and sat down beside him.

After a long few moments, Grimsley finally spoke.

"Listen, Miss Annie."

She listened. She closed her eyes and held perfectly still. Only when she became slightly light-headed did she realize that she hadn't been breathing.

"I'm sorry, Grim," she said. "I don't hear anything at all."

"Exactly," he replied. "The meadow is quiet."

"Shouldn't it be?" She was confused. "I mean, it's not like there's anybody living here."

"There are no humans who dwell in the meadow, that is true," Grimsley agreed. "But there is life. Rabbits and foxes make their homes here, as do butterflies, birds, and insects of every kind."

He shook his head. "The meadow should be filled with birdsong, the rustling of small animals, the hum of tiny wings. Something is terribly wrong."

Now that he said it, Annie realized the silence did seem strange. It was like they had placed cotton balls in their ears and then stood on a busy street. It wasn't natural for anywhere to be so still.

"Come on, Grim," she said reassuringly. "We can figure this out. If we managed to reason with a dragon and outsmart a wood elf, we can totally handle this."

She took Grimsley's paws and pulled him to his feet. They walked farther into the tall grass, searching for any clues that might tell them what was going on. They hadn't gone five feet when she heard a tiny squeaking sound from the vicinity of her ankles.

She crouched down to get a better look. Perched atop a cluster of wildflowers was a tiny girl with a thin, pointed face and electric blue hair. Delicate green wings vibrated against her back like a hummingbird's. A fairy.

Annie couldn't help her cry of astonishment. Unfortunately, this seemed to terrify the fairy, who immediately tumbled to the ground with her feet in the air. Annie picked her up, careful not to tear her fragile wings.

"Grim," she whispered. "Do fairies speak English, or do they have their own language?"

The fairy answered, in a voice that sounded strangely distorted, as if she was talking through a rolled-up piece of paper. It also sounded a little grumpy.

"The answer to both questions would be yes. And I'll thank you to address me directly from now on."

"Oh!" she cried, almost dropping the fairy in shock. "I didn't realize you could...well.... I'm really sorry," her voice trailed off awkwardly.

The fairy almost managed not to roll her eyes. Annie flushed with embarrassment.

"I didn't mean to scare you," she said. "My name is Annie…"

"I know who you are," the fairy said impatiently. "Every creature in Bibylonia knows who you are."

Now Annie was starting to get irritated. Fairy or not, this girl was kind of a brat.

"Yes, well," Annie continued, "Grim and I heard that someone here might need our help. Do you know anything about that?"

The fairy took a deep breath, looking skyward. "Use your eyes, girl," she said snippily. "The answer you seek is all around you."

Choosing to ignore the fairy's tone, she looked out at the meadow. It was just as it had been when they arrived - peaceful and still.

"I don't see anything," she said, a little more defensively than she meant to.

"Of course not!" cried the fairy. "There is nothing to see! No birds of prey searching for mice. No bees carrying pollen back to their hives. No butterflies traveling from flower to flower. We are trapped, easy prey for any creature that wanders along."

"Okay," Annie said, trying to think things through. "So, everything that can usually fly, suddenly can't?

The fairy nodded glumly.

"When did this happen?"

"Three days ago," the fairy said. "I had no warning. I simply woke in the morning and discovered that I could not fly."

"Hmmm," Annie said, puzzled, watching the fairy's wings vibrating furiously against her back. "You hadn't been hurt, or sick, or anything like that?"

"I had not," said the fairy tersely. "But…"

"Yes?" Annie prompted.

The fairy hesitated, and then continued, "I do remember, that morning, when I opened my eyes, I was suddenly struck by the strangest idea. For a moment, it was as if there was a tiny voice in my head, telling me that it was not possible for me to fly, because my body is so heavy and my wings so very small. I had never questioned how my wings could carry me, but once the idea had taken root in my mind, I could not rid myself of it."

She paced back and forth across the palm of Annie's hand, looking anxious.

"I dismissed my doubts as the lingering remnants of a nightmare, and I stepped to the edge of my flower as usual. Instead of rising, I sank like a stone to the grass below. And here I have been, ever since."

She sighed.

Annie stood up and deposited the fairy on Marty's back, causing her to splutter with indignation.

This just didn't make sense. Every time she encountered someone in Bibylonia who needed her help, there was an obvious explanation for what had happened. This seemed so random. She had a nagging feeling that she was missing something important.

"Grim," she said softly, "what will happen to them if they can't fly?"

His response came quickly; he had obviously been thinking about it too.

"At first nothing, Miss Annie. They will adapt. They will learn how to find food and shelter on the ground. They will make new homes for themselves"

Annie had not missed his phrasing. "At first?" she asked.

"Yes. Eventually, without the flying creatures carrying seeds and pollen through the air to make the flowers grow, the meadow will wither and die, and with it every source of food available to the creatures who live here. It will become a wasteland, and no creature will be able to survive here."

Annie couldn't let that happen to Grimsley's home. Reaching inside her belt pouch, her hand immediately closed over something smooth and cylindrical. Quickly she pulled it out.

It wasn't the first time she had pulled something out of the pouch without a clear idea of how it could help her. But she couldn't imagine how a bottle of bubble blowing solution was supposed to help her save the meadow. Hoping for inspiration, she climbed up on Marty's back behind the fairy and unscrewed the cap. She pulled out the little plastic wand and blew one bubble after another, watching them drift lazily across the sky. The repetitive motion seemed to settle her brain, and she began to feel less anxious.

After a few minutes, the fairy stopped pretending that Annie wasn't there and inched closer, watching the bubbles with interest. As she leaned forward to examine a particularly large one, her pointed nose pressed against the side of the bubble.

Annie expected it to pop, like normal bubbles do when exposed to, well, pretty much any object at all. Instead, this one gently bounced backwards against the wand and stuck there.

Annie poked at it lightly with her finger. Nothing happened. She pushed a little harder, with the same result. Finally, she took two fingers and squeezed on the bubble from either side. It flexed with the pressure of her fingertips, resuming its shape the moment she let go.

Annie grinned. She shook the bubble free and dipped the wand back into the bottle. Holding it a few inches away from her lips, she blew air through the center, slowly and carefully, the way her dad had taught her when she was a little girl. The result was a bubble approximately the size of her head.

Balancing it on the edge of the wand, Annie picked up the fairy with her other hand. "Here you go," she said, depositing her on top of the bubble, where she sank into its surface like a feather mattress. Annie shook the bubble gently free from the wand and into the air.

The bubble rose steadily, and the fairy's face lost its indignant expression at once. It wasn't flying, but it was close, and for now, it was enough.

"Come on, Grim," Annie called, "We've got work to do."

It took them about two hours of hunting through the tall grass, but eventually they had every butterfly, bird, bug and fairy in the meadow safely launched. There were so many bubbles in the air that the sky looked like a giant honeycomb.

Exhausted, they sat down in the grass to rest. It had taken an incredible amount of effort to round up all the creatures that were hiding, and still more to convince them that the bubbles were safe. Annie hoped she'd managed to make the bees understand how important it was to keep their stingers up. She didn't think even magical bubbles could take that kind of damage.

Together they watched the inhabitants of the meadow drift across the skyline. After a while, the blue-haired fairy wandered into their line of sight again, and Annie noticed that her bubble seemed to be growing thinner. The iridescent colors on its surface had gone rather dull, just the way bubbles did in the real world when they were about to...

Pop! The bubble winked out of existence. Annie gasped, jumping to her feet and holding out her hands to catch the fairy as she fell.

But she didn't fall. She hovered in mid-air, watching Annie curiously for a moment. Almost grudgingly, she inclined her head. Then she turned and flew away, as if the last few hours had been nothing but a dream.

They watched the rest of the bubbles pop one by one, releasing their passengers into the sky. Annie was relieved, but she also felt strangely unsettled. Everything had turned out fine, but they still didn't know why it had happened in the first place.

"I don't understand it, Miss Annie," Grimsley said, getting to his feet. "They were able to fly all along, or they would not have been able to stay aloft when the bubbles burst."

"I know, it doesn't make any sense. What could make a fairy forget how to fly?"

"That would be me."

The voice came from behind them. It was mild, even pleasant, but the fine hairs on the back of Annie's neck rose at the sound of it. She turned her head slowly, afraid of what she might see.

The man who stood there was not unusual in any way. In fact, he was very nearly as average as someone can be. He wasn't fat, but he wasn't thin either. He was neither particularly tall, nor terribly short. His hair was an ordinary shade of brown, neatly cut, and his facial features were even and regular. Dressed in a plain white tee shirt and blue jeans, he was the kind of person you could walk past in a crowd and later you would never remember that you had seen him at all.

There was nothing threatening about his posture as he stood there with his hands in his pockets, smiling. Annie couldn't understand why her blood was suddenly roaring in her ears.

The man took a step forward, and Annie instinctively stepped back. He chuckled, and the sound sent the sensation of stinging ants down her arms.

"Now, Miss Annie," he said gently. "I mean you no harm."

He began to walk towards her. The closer he got, the less he looked like an actual man. He moved just a little too quickly, with funny occasional hitches, like you might see in an old movie. His features were all where they should be, but there was a wrongness about them, as if he was wearing an ill-fitting mask that didn't quite map to the face underneath. Even his clothes looked strange, shifting fluidly as he walked.

Annie kept backing up until she bumped into something warm and unyielding; Marty. She looked around wildly for Grimsley and found him huddled on the ground behind the tiger, rocking back and forth like a child.

"Y-you did this?" she whispered. "You made them forget they could fly?"

The man nodded.

"Why?" she asked. Her instincts told her she should be running instead of asking questions, but she wasn't sure her legs would hold her weight.

He laughed, a hearty belly laugh this time. Her stomach twisted as if she'd been punched.

"Oh, dear girl," he said merrily. "I would have thought that would be obvious. To see what would happen, of course."

He put two fingers in his mouth and made a high-pitched whistling sound. It was immediately followed by the unmistakable clattering of hooves.

At first, the animal that appeared on the hill behind them looked like a horse. It was pale grey, with a twisted horn on its brow. A unicorn, then. But this was not like any unicorn she'd ever seen in one of her books.

Its horn was broken about halfway down, and the jagged edge looked as sharp as one of her mother's kitchen knives. Patches of its hide were completely worn away, exposing a framework of rusty wire and empty air beneath. It was like a child's toy that had been left in the attic for the moths to eat. Its eyelids were closed and sunken. Annie had no idea how it could see where it was going. Perhaps it was simply following the sound of the man's voice – it moved quickly and unerringly down the path towards him.

It couldn't possibly be alive, but somehow it was walking. Its sides contracted and expanded in a parody of breath. As it grew closer, an overwhelming smell invaded Annie's nostrils, penetrating so deeply that it dropped her to her knees; rotten garbage and something else she couldn't identify, sickly sweet and nauseating. Marty put his paws over his nose in protest.

Holding onto its tattered mane with one hand, the man swung himself up onto the unicorn's back. He tipped an imaginary hat to Annie before turning to ride off over the hill and out of sight.

Marty butted his head against her back, whining. She reached down and put both arms around his neck, as much for her own comfort as his. After the man had been gone for several minutes, Grimsley crawled out from behind the tiger, although he seemed reluctant to move away from the big cat completely.

Clinging to Marty's side, his terrified face only inches from hers, he whispered hoarsely, "What was that, Miss Annie?"

Annie stared at the empty space where the man had been, wishing she had the answer to that excellent question.

CHAPTER 28
THE COUNCIL OF GUARDIANS RECONVENES

After leaving the meadow, Annie felt an almost overwhelming need to return to the garden. Her interest in further adventure that night had completely evaporated. The encounter with the strange man made her feel vulnerable in a way that nothing in this dream world ever had.

She opened the gate with trembling hands and hurried through it, leaving a very worried Grimsley on the other side. Racing down the garden path, she reached the wooden door that would take her home and pushed it open without a backwards glance.

She was still asleep an hour later when the Council of Guardians descended on her abandoned dollhouse for the second time.

They were very agitated, and this made them far less cautious than they would normally have been about the amount of noise they were making. They paced through the tiny rooms, bumping into walls and speaking anxiously to each other in rapidly rising voices. Marty's paw appeared beneath the bedroom door, swiping back and forth in a desperate attempt to reach the intruders.

The Lady appeared at the edge of the dollhouse's overcrowded living room, leaning heavily on her walking stick as she surveyed her council. She looked tired. She rapped the stick sharply on the floor to get their attention, and they quieted immediately.

"By now you have all heard the rumors." she addressed the crowd. "Indeed, I would be amazed if there is a single creature in Bibylonia who has not heard them, so quickly have they traveled these past few days."

There were nods and whispers of agreement from the crowd.

"Much as I would like to tell you they are only stories," she said gravely,

"I cannot."

The Guardians looked stunned. It was clear that no matter how anxious they had been, most of them had been expecting reassurance from their leader, some indication that their fears were unfounded.

"Something has risen from the mists of the Grey Plains," the Lady went on. "It walks and talks, and it resembles a man, though it is not one. Grimsley tells me that he and Annie encountered this creature in the sacred meadow today."

All eyes turned to Grimsley, who was standing at the edge of the dollhouse, apart from the other Guardians. He did not take his own eyes from the Lady's.

"Perhaps," suggested the snake-haired girl who had spoken at the last council meeting, in a quavering voice, "if we sent the child home and barred her from returning…"

The Lady shook her head. "Once made, life cannot be easily unmade," she replied. "Whether or not he was ever intended to have life, he has it now."

"Then what shall we do?" the girl asked, despairingly.

"We will watch," the old woman said quietly, "and we will wait."

And with that she vanished, leaving the bewildered Council behind.

The silence was broken by all of the Guardians suddenly talking at once. Some were in favor of immediately preparing for battle. Others contended that if they could find out what he wanted, they could send the man back to the Grey Plains with it and have it end there. Grimsley didn't engage in these debates. He had seen first-hand what the man could do. And he didn't think he had any interest in going home.

Annie stirred restlessly in her bed as their arguments grew louder. When a mermaid swept a tiny lamp from its table with an angry flick of her tail, it fell to the floor with a crash, echoing through the room like cannon fire.

Annie sat up, now fully awake. The panicked Guardians leapt to the floor, running across the room as fast as they could go. Annie's eyes, still adjusting to the darkness, failed to pick out their tiny forms as they sought the safety of the bookshelf, and their way home.

Just as she had decided that the noise must have come from outside, there was another loud crash. She jumped out of bed, nearly tripping over a pile of paperbacks on the floor. She picked one up to put it back on the shelf. Underneath was the tiny, trembling form of a rabbit, no bigger than the palm of her hand. A rabbit wearing a very familiar eyepatch and black boots.

Grimsley.

CHAPTER 29
THE DREAMER AWAKENS

She stood up and flicked on the overhead light. Blinded, Grimsley buried his face in his paws. She sat down again, holding him up in her cupped hands.

"I'm not in Bibylonia, am I?" Annie asked, although she already knew the answer.

Grimsley shook his head miserably.

"I don't understand. Is this some other kind of dream? And why are you so small?"

To Annie's astonishment, Grimsley began to cry. Fat tears streamed silently down his face, pooling briefly in her fingers before dripping down onto the floor.

"No, Miss Annie," he said at last. "This is not a dream."

"But…"

"I am small because that is the only way I can travel through the portal that connects our homes. And I am here because I am tired, and frightened, and clumsy. I tripped over my own boots in my attempt to reach the bookcase. It was my stumble that caused the books to fall and you to wake."

"But…if I'm actually here, and you're actually here…"

Annie knew what the logical conclusion was, but she couldn't bring herself to say the words. In the end, Grimsley did it for her.

"Bibylonia is real, Miss Annie," he said quietly. "Had you Called when you were older, you would have been told that from the start. Because you were so young, the Lady deemed it necessary to let you believe you were dreaming, at least at first."

Annie leaned against the wall. On the one hand, it was the most ridiculous thing she had ever heard. On the other, she was sitting on her floor talking to a rabbit.

"Okay," she said slowly, "if I haven't gone completely crazy, what were you doing in my room in the first place?

"The Council convened after…after the meadow, to decide what to do."

"Why did you have to come here? Why couldn't you just meet in the forest?"

Grimsley hesitated. "That is our usual custom, Miss Annie," he said. "The Council has met in your world only twice. The first time, we gathered here so that we might unlock the door that leads to your garden, so that you could cross over into Bibylonia for the first time.

Tonight," he continued, not meeting her eyes, "we came so that if the Lady willed it, we could seal the door again and prevent you from returning."

Annie felt all the blood rush from her face at once. "But…why?"

"Because of the man, Miss Annie," he said sadly. "The man from the meadow."

"Because I didn't fight him?" she whispered. "I know that's supposed to be my job, but Grim, I…I think I'm way out of my league with this guy."

She didn't want to say the next words, but she knew she had to.

"I don't think I'm brave enough."

Grimsley put his tiny paw over her hand and squeezed it.

"If the Council had chosen to seal the door, it would not have been because you are not brave, Miss Annie, but because you are the reason the man came to be."

At first, the only thing she heard was that she was not banned from returning to Bibylonia. Relief flooded her, slowing her frantic heartbeat. Only when she realized Grimsley's miserable expression had not changed did the meaning of the rest of his words sink in.

"No," she responded vehemently. "No way. I may have imagined Bibylonia into existence, and now that I know it's a real place, I'm not sure I even believe that anymore, but I have no idea where that man came from!"

Grimsley just looked at her, his face both serious and sad.

"Come on, Grim," she pleaded. "You have to believe me."

"Everything in Bibylonia came from you, Miss Annie," he reminded her gently. "There is no village or town, no creature walking that did not have its beginnings in your imagination."

"But I've never even seen anything like him before!" she cried. "I mean, I know where I first saw you, and the other Guardians too. Books, and movies, even stories I made up in my head, but…"

The memory made goosebumps rise on her arms. "I don't think I could ever have imagined something like that."

"We all know that you would never intentionally do such a thing, Miss Annie. Otherwise, the Lady would certainly have given orders to block your return. But the fact remains," he continued with a heavy sigh, "that he lives, and the world is in great danger."

Annie tried to take in this overwhelming information. Her last thought upon leaving her garden that night had been that the man must have been some kind of glitch in her dream, like an error in a computer program. Surely when she went back to Bibylonia he would be gone, and everything would be back to normal. But, from what Grimsley was saying, he was there to stay. And it was her fault.

CHAPTER 30
NUMB

Annie hadn't been able to go back to sleep after Grimsley had disappeared through her bookcase to Bibylonia and had spent the remainder of the night pacing her room, trying to figure out what to do. As a result, her eyes were ringed with red and she burst into tears when her alarm went off in the morning. Her mother took one look at her and hustled her off to the pediatrician's office.

The doctor couldn't find anything wrong with her, of course, but she recommended that Annie take the day off from school, to be on the safe side. Back home, her mother tucked her into bed before heading downstairs to leave for work, instructing her to call for her father if she needed anything.

Because her door was ajar, Annie could hear the quiet conversation between her parents at the foot of the stairs. Apparently, Annie's math teacher had called the evening before, concerned about the fact that her grade had dropped from an A to a C in just a few weeks.

Annie had been finding it increasingly difficult to concentrate in class since the twins had stepped up their campaign of intimidation, and she had known it was only a matter of time before her grades started to slip as a result. Ordinarily the very idea of a C would have made Annie hyperventilate, but right now she all she wanted was to go back to Bibylonia so that she could find out what was happening. As tired as she was, she couldn't fall asleep. She lay in bed for hours, wide awake and staring at the ceiling.

Her mother came home early that afternoon. Annie heard Maisy galloping up the stairs and quickly turned to face the wall. She didn't want to talk to anyone right now, especially not an annoying four-year-old. She heard her sister push the door to her room open and whisper her name. Annie pretended to be asleep until she went away.

Annie reluctantly crawled out of bed. She would need to call Jay to get the day's assignments, and he ought to be home by now. She pulled on a sweatshirt and went downstairs to retrieve the phone.

When she walked into the kitchen, her parents were sitting close together, talking in hushed voices. They stopped when she entered the room and looked up with such guilty expressions that she knew she had interrupted a conversation about her.

"Hey," she said. "I'm feeling a little better, so I was going to call Jay about the homework."

"Good idea," her dad replied. "I think the phone is still in the study from my last conference call. I need to make sure your sister isn't blowing anything up in the playroom anyway, so I'll get it for you."

He got up, exchanging a meaningful glance with her mother before heading down the hallway.

Annie knew what that look meant. It was time for an 'important talk' and her mother had been designated to deliver it.

Sure enough, the first thing her mother said was, "Sit down, Annie."

Annie had a pretty good idea what this conversation was going to be about and also that she wasn't going to like it. She sat.

"We got a phone call from Mr. Walliford last night," her mother began.

"Yeah, I know," Annie said. "I heard you and Dad talking about it this morning."

Annie knew she should say something else, try to explain why her grade had dropped so significantly, but the words just wouldn't come.

Her mother looked at her strangely. "He says you're not paying attention in class, Annie. That you're turning in unfinished homework. That's not something I've ever heard from a teacher before. What can you tell me about why that's happening?"

Annie looked down at her lap. She didn't know what to say. She was screwing up everything, in both worlds, and she didn't have any better idea of how to fix things here than she did in Bibylonia.

The minutes that passed before her mom spoke again seemed to last for years.

"I wish you would just talk to me," she said, finally. "I know there's something going on with you, no matter how often you tell me there isn't."

Annie looked up and saw that her mother had tears in her eyes, something that had happened only a handful of times in Annie's memory. She leaned over and pressed a hand against Annie's face.

"Please," she said, urgently. "Tell me how I can help you."

Annie probably would have told her mother everything right then, no matter what the consequences might be. But it was at that moment that her father appeared at the door, a stricken look on his face, and what looked like a tangle of yarn dangling from his hand.

"I'm so sorry, Annie," he said sadly. "It's my fault. I left the scissors on my desk when I came in to talk to your mother. I didn't leave her alone for long, but…"

He held out his hand like an apology, and Annie finally realized what he was holding; the remains of Miss Kitty. Maisy must have taken her out of Annie's room while she had been pretending to be asleep.

Annie walked over to her father and took Miss Kitty from his hand. It was obvious that she wasn't fixable. Stuffing fell like snowflakes onto the kitchen floor and there weren't enough whole pieces left to tell a leg from a tail.

She had been sleeping with that stuffed cat since she was two. Her parents frequently joked that Annie would take it to college with her. She should have been furious, she should have been inconsolably sad, but the destruction of Miss Kitty didn't even register beside the overwhelming feeling that she was losing everything in the world that mattered to her.

She opened the cabinet under the sink and put Miss Kitty's mangled body in the trash. She turned around to face her parents, who were watching her with shocked expressions.

"It's okay, Dad. I'm getting too old for stuffed animals, anyway."

She turned and walked out of the kitchen. In her room, she climbed back into bed, pulled the covers over her head, and waited for night to fall.

CHAPTER 31
UNDER SIEGE

Annie knew something was wrong in the garden before she even opened her eyes. The moss she lay upon, usually soft as velvet, felt crisp and fragile beneath her cheek. When she sat up, she saw that it was no longer green but bleached yellow, like grass in the dead of winter.

Looking around, she saw dying plants everywhere. The tiny blue flowers that had crept across the path were withered and brown. The giant sunflowers drooped on their skyscraper stems; their blooms crumpled in the dirt. Marty nosed at one of them, growling softly.

The only thing thriving was the ivy, which had grown so rapidly that it now completely obscured the garden walls. But even that was different. The delicate white blooms that had dotted the vines were gone, and the usually bright green leaves were almost black. They looked healthy when nothing else in the garden did, but they also looked poisonous.

She stepped onto the path, feeling a twinge of sadness for the giggling irises that had once blocked the way. She headed towards the clearing, nearly unrecognizable without the glorious pink flowers draped over its entrance.

It was empty. For the first time since she had discovered Bibylonia, Grimsley was not in the garden to greet her. She returned to the main garden and headed towards the gate. Once she finally managed to peel the ivy free from the lock, she was surprised to find that the formerly gleaming metal had rusted overnight. When she drew out her key on its long silver chain, she saw that it also looked like it had been left outside for years. She hoped it would still turn the lock.

The gate did open with a little effort, creaking like a loose floorboard. She locked it behind her and tucked the key back inside her shirt. After the whirlwind had done its work, she climbed onto Marty's back and set off, her eyes raking the trees for any sign of Grimsley or the other Guardians, but they were nowhere to be found. The only sign of life was a black squirrel darting across the forest floor.

When she reached the edge of the forest, she discovered why it was so quiet. The Guardians, all of the Guardians, were positioned at the tree line, standing a few feet apart. Off in the distance she spotted a familiar pair of tall pointy ears. She pulled on Marty's neck to show him where to go, and he took off as fast as he could run.

He skidded to a halt in front of Grimsley, dragging his tongue affectionately across the rabbit's face. Grimsley tried to maintain a serious expression but couldn't manage it; he smiled and rumpled the tiger's ears.

"Hey, Grim," she said, "what's going on?" She gestured at the other Guardians.

"We have been called away from our usual duties to defend the forest," he explained.

"Against the man?"

He nodded.

"Has he been here?" she asked, feeling a flutter of panic at the idea of the man coming so close to her garden.

"Not yet, Miss Annie," he said anxiously. "But the Lady says he will come, so we wait."

Maybe since they had all the Guardians together, they could just...what? Put him in jail? She wasn't even sure there was anything like a jail in Bibylonia. It wasn't something she had ever thought about. But they couldn't do anything if they didn't even know where he was.

And then it hit her.

"Grim," she said urgently, "I need the map."

He blinked.

"The map," she repeated. "The one we use to figure out who needs our help. We have to find out where the man is to fight him, and wherever he is, the people there are definitely going to need help."

For a long few moments, he simply looked at her. Then he shook his head and said quietly, "I can't."

"What?" Annie gaped at him in disbelief. "But, but...you've got to."

Her throat closed around the words she needed to say next, but she managed to force them out. "It's my fault, Grim."

"I can't," he repeated. "If I do, it will be my fault."

"What will?"

But he bent his head and refused to say another word.

Desperate, Annie stepped forward and put her hands on Grimsley's shoulders.

"Listen," she said, "I just want to find out where he is and what he's doing. Then I'll come back and tell the Lady and you guys can do whatever you need to do to stop him."

Grimsley still looked dubious, but he was at least looking at her now instead of his boots.

"I'll use the map to find him, check it out on Marty, and come right back. I'll never even get close to him, I swear.

Grim, please," she pleaded. "I...I have to do something."

Without taking his eyes from Annie's face, he reached into his boot and withdrew the familiar parchment. Annie took it quickly, before he could change his mind, spreading it out on the ground in front of her.

Before the paper had even completely unfurled, a section of the map blazed to life like a campfire. Annie pulled her hand back from the intensity of the heat. Sucking on her scorched fingers, she knelt down to find the source of the sudden flare-up.

Aesoppla.

It was all she could do not to leap on Marty's back and ride away at once. He was in Aesoppla. Where Clarence was. And Mrs. Otter. They couldn't protect themselves against a group of mischievous wood elves; they would be totally defenseless against the man.

Her heart pounding, she flung both arms around Grimsley and buried her face in his soft neck. He hugged her back and they stood there for a long moment. Finally, she let go and handed the map back to Grimsley. She knew where the man was. She didn't need it anymore.

CHAPTER 32
TROUBLE AT THE TOURNAMENT

Although the bell in the clock tower was pealing merrily when Annie rode into town, Aesoppla was otherwise oddly still. There were no alligators on bicycles today, and the park benches were empty. Even the shops were closed. Annie's sense of disquiet grew. Surely there should be someone out and about.

Remembering the location of the town hall from her previous visit, she guided Marty towards the large brick building in the center of the village square. When they got close to it, Annie could see a sign posted above the tall double doors. She jumped off the tiger's back and ran to get a better look.

"All-Aesoppla Chess Tournament – Final Match Today at 10:30 AM," she read, her shoulders sagging with relief. Of course. Clarence had told them it was coming up soon. She and Grimsley had even planned to attend before everything had happened with the man. That must be where everyone was – watching the tournament.

But, a nagging voice in her head countered, the clock was chiming twelve just a few moments ago. Everyone in Aesoppla eats lunch at exactly noon; Mrs. Otter had told her that. Would they really let the match run over and risk being off schedule for the rest of the day?

Unfortunately, Annie knew the answer to that question, and her certainty that something was seriously wrong returned. She took a deep breath and pushed open the doors.

She found herself facing a cavernous room, high-ceilinged and perfectly square. Tall windows lined the walls, and sunlight streamed through them onto the gleaming wooden floors.

There were dozens of long narrow tables, all pushed against the walls except for one, which had been placed in the center of the room. Upon it sat a chess board, clearly abandoned in the middle of a game. Several of the pieces lay scattered on the floor.

Annie had a moment to wonder where the players had gone before her attention was drawn to the far side of the room by a loud hissing sound, like air being forced out of a giant rubber ball. All she could see from where she stood was a great stone fireplace, and a group of animals huddled around it. Knowing that she would find nothing good when she got there, she nevertheless began to run.

Even when she reached the crowd, she couldn't immediately see what was happening through the forest of legs in front of her. Finding a narrow gap between a wolf and a flock of flamingos, Annie shifted sideways and squeezed her body through. Marty sent the wolf sprawling across the floor with his giant head as he followed.

On the floor in front of the fireplace were two animals, one thrashing wildly, the other perfectly still. One of them she knew very well, and she realized who the other must be with a sinking feeling in her stomach.

Several animals she recognized from the clock-keeper's house were struggling to hold Clarence's writhing body to the ground. That was where the horrible hissing sound was coming from. At first Annie thought the cobra was trying to attack the animals holding him, but upon closer inspection it didn't look that way. His head whipped back and forth, and his face was contorted in pain. Whenever he caught sight of the motionless form of the mongoose on the floor, who could only be his best friend Bob, the hissing noise grew louder. Annie suddenly realized that Clarence was crying.

She turned towards the nearest animal, a sleek black panther.

"What happened?" she asked urgently.

"We do not know, Miss Annie," he replied, never taking his eyes from the struggling snake. "The game ended with Clarence the victor, which is not unusual. Bob had just begun to offer congratulations when the doors opened, and a man walked in."

Not just a man, Annie thought. The man.

"The newcomer congratulated Clarence on his victory, though how he would know anything about the game with such a late arrival, I do not know. He left as quickly as he came."

The panther turned to face her, frowning.

"If I hadn't seen it with my own eyes, I would never have believed it," he said. "No sooner had the doors closed behind the stranger than Clarence lunged forward and sank his fangs into Bob's shoulder."

"But," Annie was appalled, "they're best friends. Why would Clarence do something like that?"

The panther shook his head. "That is what we do not understand. When his bite didn't disable Bob, he resorted to using his tail, wrapping it tightly around Bob's neck. At that point several of the clock-keeper's guards stepped in."

"Is he...," Annie was afraid to finish her question.

"He is alive," the panther replied, "but only just. The medics are on their way, and they will do what they can."

Annie stepped forward and crouched in front of the mongoose. Clarence was right, he was a funny-looking creature. She remembered the cobra's happy description of their unlikely friendship. How could things possibly have gone so very wrong?

Clarence's agonized hissing suddenly stopped, replaced by a pitiful wail. She looked up to see the guards pulling the cobra away from the crowd. He was straining his entire body in Bob's direction.

Annie stood up, intending to try to at least offer Clarence some comfort; to tell him that she knew he would never intentionally hurt his friend. But she never got the chance.

She hadn't taken a single step when he suddenly reared up to his full height, breaking free of the guards holding him. His hood flared and he hissed again, a very different sound than the one he'd made before. This was an angry sound, a dangerous sound, and it was unmistakably directed at her.

Annie froze, racking her brain for what could have made Clarence forget they were friends, that he was a police officer, not a predator.

And then, the smell hit her. Garbage left out in the hot sun, overwhelming even in the large room. Even though she'd only encountered it once before, she knew immediately where it was coming from.

CHAPTER 33
WHAT ANYONE WANTS

The man leaned casually against the frame of the open door. The source of the smell, his nightmare unicorn, paced restlessly outside.

He nodded pleasantly at Annie, as if they were passing each other on the sidewalk instead of standing only feet from a murderous giant snake. It was just the way he had behaved back in the meadow, like there was nothing unusual about what was happening.

She didn't know how he was doing it, but he was the reason Clarence had gone on a rampage. If she could only get Clarence far enough away from the man, maybe he would come to his senses.

But how was she supposed to make a giant snake go somewhere he didn't want to go? He was too strong for her to handle on her own, and the other animals were too busy keeping him from killing anyone to be much help to her.

Unless...

She turned to the panther. "I have an idea," she told him, "but I need the clock-keeper's help. Can you find him for me?"

Without hesitation, the panther turned and raced across the room, bounding out a back door she hadn't noticed when she came in.

"Hang in there, Clarence," she whispered. "Help is on the way."

It was probably only a few minutes before the panther returned, but to Annie it felt like hours. Hours spent staring into Clarence's eyes with no one she recognized looking back at her. He made no further attempt to strike, but Annie had never in her life felt so much like prey.

The clock-keeper entered the room, his cane tapping on the wooden floor as he approached. When he had almost reached her, Annie lunged towards the table where the ill-fated chess match had been played and grabbed one of the high-backed chairs, dragging it quickly out of the cobra's reach. She helped the beaver into the chair and gently removed the cane from his paws. Surprised, he looked up at her.

"I promise I'll bring it back, but right now it's our only chance," she assured him.

He studied the cane for a moment, and then looked at Clarence. He nodded and settled back into the chair to wait.

Holding the cane in front of her like a sword, Annie stepped towards the angry snake. His eyes followed her as she moved.

As quickly as she could, she darted behind him, extending the curved handle of the cane around his body just below the hood, hooking it firmly around his neck, just like she'd seen snake handlers do in the videos she'd watched with Jay. One of the animals that had been restraining Clarence, an enormous grizzly bear, reached out and took the cane from her grasp. The rest of the animals gathered around to help. With the cane hooked around his neck, they were able to use their combined strength to drag the enormous snake towards the back door.

"I think he'll be himself again after you get him out of here," she told the bear. "Get him as far away as possible; take him home if you can. See if his mother will turn on the TV for him, even if it's the wrong time of day for it. And tell him…," Annie swallowed hard, "that we'll do everything we can to help Bob."

The grizzly nodded, and then they were through the door and gone.

Annie tried to push down the knot of worry in the pit of her stomach. She was pretty sure Clarence would be all right once he was far enough away from the man, but what if she was wrong?

The silence was broken by the sound of slow, deliberate applause. Annie whirled around. In her desperation to get her friend to a safe place, she had nearly forgotten that the danger itself remained in the room. With her.

The man was still standing in the doorway, a genuine smile of delight on his face. It was this smile, more than anything else that had happened so far, that made it hard to stand her ground and not run away. But she couldn't leave the animals of Aesoppla to face the man alone.

A quick glance told her the panther stood close by. She whispered as quietly as she could, knowing that cats had remarkable hearing.

"Take the others and run," she said. "Go to the wood elves and ask them to take you in. Speak to Will Sykes - tell him I sent you."

She turned to face the man, who stood with his hands clasped in front of him, regarding her like a proud parent at a child's recital.

Behind her, Annie could hear the animals stampeding out the back door. Finally, only she and the man remained. She wondered where Marty had gone. She hoped he had fled with the others - she didn't think she could bear it if anything happened to him.

"Well done, Miss Annie," the man beamed at her. "You kept the cobra from killing anyone, although he dearly wanted to. And you sent the others to safety. Well," he amended, "to relative safety at any rate. I must say, you've been terribly brave and clever."

Annie would have laughed if she hadn't been so terrified. If there had ever been a time she felt less brave and clever, she didn't know when it had been.

The man still hadn't moved, but Annie was gripped by the sudden fear that he would do so at any moment. She wasn't sure what would happen if he touched her, but she knew it wouldn't be good. She had to think of a way to distract him, to keep him where he was.

"Who are you?" she asked.

It seemed to take him by surprise. His brows knitted together, and his head tilted to one side.

"Who am I?" he repeated. "What an interesting question."

He rubbed his chin thoughtfully. "I don't know that I've ever had a name. I have always simply been."

He smiled suddenly. "You may call me John," he said cheerfully. "John Doe. It suits me, don't you think? After all, I'm really just an ordinary fellow."

He laughed, and Annie felt suddenly cold, despite the warmth of the fire.

She had to keep him talking.

"What do you want?"

He nodded approvingly. "Another excellent question! I do so enjoy children; everything is so direct. 'Who are you?' 'What do you want?' Really, it saves so much time."

The man opened his arms wide in a gesture of solidarity.

"I want what anyone wants, of course. What you want, in fact."

She stared at him. She couldn't imagine that she shared anything in common with this creature.

He smiled gently at her confusion.

"I want life," he said. "A life where I can truly be myself. Where I can do the things that make me happy. Isn't that why you came to Bibylonia in the first place?"

His words stung. Yes, that was why she had come here, but what made her happy was fixing things. While she still didn't really understand what he was doing or why, it seemed like wherever John Doe went, bad things happened.

"You can help me, Miss Annie," he continued. "That's what you do, isn't it, help people?"

"I won't help you," she said angrily. "Why would I, after what you just did to Clarence?"

"Because," he said patiently, "if you will just give me what I want, I will leave Bibylonia, and never return."

Annie sucked in a breath. It was exactly what she wanted; a way to rid Bibylonia of the man once and for all. Grimsley and the others would be safe, and she could finally stop feeling as if she had brought destruction down on their heads.

"What would I have to do?" she asked warily.

"Almost nothing," he said lightly. "Simply give me that key you wear around your neck, and I shall be gone so quickly that I will barely register as a memory."

Give him her key? But that would mean...

"You want to leave Bibylonia?"

He bent forward in a graceful half bow.

"Rather funny, isn't it? All you want is to be allowed to stay here, and all I want is to leave. What I am suggesting is something in the nature of a trade. Leave behind the home you find so tedious and ordinary and stay here in Bibylonia forever, living out your...dreams."

He chuckled at his own humor.

"In exchange, I will remain in your world. There are so many opportunities to explore - I can't imagine I would ever grow bored there."

He stood, hands in his pockets, waiting for her response, as much at ease as if they had been talking about the weather.

She would be lying if she said she didn't consider it, just for a moment. If you had asked her yesterday what she wanted more than anything, she would have said that she never wanted to go back to school. That she never wanted to be that Annie again, the one who walked through the corridors with her head down and her eyes on the floor. She wanted to be the Annie who always knew what to do. She wanted to be strong.

That was what the man was offering her now, the opportunity to become that person forever. All she had to do to make it happen was abandon her family and friends, and send them a monster in her place. And that was most definitely not something a hero would do.

"Forget it," she said firmly, folding her arms and trying to look less petrified than she felt. She tried to picture exactly how far behind her the back door stood so that she could make a run for it if he started towards her.

But he didn't. He simply shrugged his shoulders, as if he had received exactly the answer he had expected.

"Have it your way," he replied. "For now, at any rate."

Without another word, he turned and strolled out the front door. He swung himself onto the unicorn's back with an easy grace. Annie watched as he rode slowly down one of the cobblestoned streets towards the edge of town. As they turned the corner, she saw him raise his hand in farewell, and she recognized the gesture for what it was.

A warning.

Annie raced to the back door and threw it open. Outside she found a narrow sunlit street lined with rows of tiny houses, just the right size for a family of birds, and Marty, cowering behind a giant tree that was nevertheless too small to completely hide him from view.

She ran to him, burying her face in his fur. She was so grateful to find him safe; she wasn't sure which of them was trembling more.

"Come on, boy," she said, climbing on his back. "I think we're going to need some help."

Marty didn't need additional encouragement. As soon as Annie was settled, he took off down the path at a run, anxious to put as much distance between them and John Doe as possible.

CHAPTER 34
THE FOREST AND THE TREE

Annie's thoughts were racing as Marty's paws pounded along the path. She had no idea what she was going to do next, only that she had to get back to Grimsley. She almost cried with relief when she spotted the Guardians, still standing along the edge of the trees. She had been half afraid that she would find the forest in the same state as Aesoppla, but it didn't appear that John Doe had found his way here yet. He would, if he wanted into her world. It was only a matter of time.

Marty spotted Grimsley before she did, skidding sideways to correct his course. Any other time Annie would have been howling with laughter at the expression on Grimsley's face when he realized there was a five-hundred-pound tiger barreling towards him at top speed. Today, all she could feel was relief that her friend was still safe from the danger she had brought into his world.

She was off Marty's back before he had come to a complete stop, stumbling into Grimsley and almost knocking him to the ground.

"Miss Annie," Grimsley said, startled. "What has happened?"

Annie told him. Grimsley's expression grew increasingly anxious as she spoke, and the comforting arm he had placed around her shoulder shook so badly that Annie's own teeth were chattering.

"I think," said Grimsley when she had finished, "that it is time for you to speak with the Lady."

Annie stared up into her friend's serious face.

"Take me to her," she replied.

They walked in silence, stepping over rotten logs and drifts of fallen leaves. They were deep in the forest when Grimsley finally stopped in front of the biggest oak tree Annie had ever seen. Ten people holding hands wouldn't have been able to circle its trunk, and its thick branches created a curtain of leaves that blocked all but occasional glimpses of the sky overhead. Looking up at it, Annie had the strangest feeling that the tree was watching her. She knew that all trees were alive, but she thought maybe this one was a little more "alive" than most.

Grimsley knocked three times on the tree's gnarled trunk. A loud echoing sound followed. Then, a woman's voice responded from inside the tree.

"Come in, please."

"The Lady will see you now," Grimsley told her.

"Um," she said, sure she must be missing something obvious. "Is there a door somewhere?"

Grimsley took her hand and placed it against the tree. "Remember that you made this place, Miss Annie. There is nowhere in Bibylonia that is closed to you."

Annie felt like a complete idiot standing with her hand against the tree. She had no idea what she was supposed to do. She closed her eyes. I want to come in, she thought, as hard as she could.

She felt the tree twitch, and her eyes flew open in surprise. Her fingers were splayed against a bright blue door set into the tree trunk, perfectly round, and exactly the right size to admit an eleven-year-old girl. She pushed gently on the door and stepped inside.

CHAPTER 35
AN AUDIENCE WITH THE LADY

The door closed silently behind her as she stepped inside. She was in a small, high-ceilinged room, as perfectly round as the tree itself. In the center of the room sat an old-fashioned cast-iron wood stove and two high-backed rocking chairs. The only other furniture was a tiny bed, about the right size for a child, and a rickety set of shelves overflowing with haphazard piles of dusty books, copper pots, and old shoes. Annie instantly felt at home, even though the room was as different from her own house as it was possible to be.

A flash of movement caught her eye from outside one of the many windows that lined the walls. Strange, she thought. How could there be windows on the inside of a tree?

She walked over to the one closest to her and peered out. She drew back in surprise, recognizing the ivy strangled walls of her own garden. Looking through the next she was astonished to see the deserted streets of Aesoppla.

She moved quickly through the room, looking through each window in turn. There was the sacred meadow, teeming with life now the way it was intended to. Next were the Guardians standing at the edge of the forest, on constant alert for any sign of John Doe. And there...

There was the man himself, riding slowly through a cluster of small houses and farms. A town was just visible in the distance, and it was one that Annie recognized; the village of Grimm that had been the site of her first adventure in Bibylonia.

"No!" she cried, beating her fist on the window frame. "Get away from there!"

John Doe's head turned slowly as if he could hear her, as impossible as that seemed. He smiled in her direction before returning his focus to the little town that lay ahead.

Annie backed away from the window, searching frantically for a way out. She had to get to Grimm and try to stop the man from doing whatever it was he was about to do.

Just then, she heard the unmistakable sound of someone clearing their throat. She whipped her head around, looking for the source of the noise. One of the chairs by the fire shifted to face her, and she saw the old woman seated in it.

She was no bigger than a child, which was probably why Annie hadn't noticed her in the first place. She held an enormous book open in her lap and a small grey cat tucked into the crook of her arm, its head barely visible.

"There is nothing you can do," the Lady said calmly. "He has already reached the town square. The citizens of Grimm will have to do the best they can."

She closed the book, reaching for the walking stick that was hanging from a hook on the side of the wood stove. She rose to her feet, sending the cat streaking away under the bed.

"Who knows," she added, "they may very well find themselves up to the task. After all, they have faced great danger once before and lived to tell the tale."

One of these days, if they all managed to get through this, Annie was going to make Grimsley tell her that fairy godmother story.

The old woman lifted a tray with a child-sized china tea service down from its precarious perch on top of the stove. Tea bags were already nestled in two of the cups. It was almost as if the Lady had known she would be coming.

"Sit down, Anneliese."

Feeling a little nervous, Annie sat in one of the rocking chairs. The teacups tipped back and forth on the tray like a seesaw as the old woman poured the hot water, threatening to topple at any moment. Handing Annie one of the cups and returning the tray to the stove, she settled in the other chair, rocking it slowly back and forth with the end of her walking stick.

Unable to stand the silence, Annie spoke.

"Lady," she said, "I've just returned from Aesoppla."

"I know."

"You...do?"

The Lady nodded in the direction of the windows.

"You did well, child. Faced with great risk to your own safety, you acted first to protect your friend. In doing so, you not only saved your own life, but spared Clarence the overwhelming guilt that would have been his lifelong companion had he killed you."

"What happened to him?" Annie asked. "I know it has something to do with the man, but I don't really understand. I mean, he didn't do anything to Clarence, at least not while I was there. And the panther said all he did before I got there was congratulate Clarence on winning the game. He didn't cast a spell on him. He didn't even touch him!"

"He does not need weapons or enchantments to lay his victims low," the Lady said, stirring her tea. "That is the nature of his gift."

She placed her cup on the floor and leaned back in her chair. The cat, which had re-emerged from beneath the bed, leapt lightly onto her lap again, watching Annie with bright yellow eyes.

"I'm sorry, Lady," Annie said. "What is his gift, exactly?"

"John Doe is an empath, Annie, a very powerful one."

That wasn't a word Annie knew. She looked blankly at the Lady, who smiled kindly in return.

"An empath is uniquely sensitive to other people's emotions. There are many who claim to have this gift, both in your world and in ours, but they rely heavily on the physical cues that people provide to know what they are feeling. This is not what I mean."

She rose from her seat, sending the irritated cat skittering across the floor again. Leaning on her cane, she walked slowly towards the window facing Grimm. Annie followed.

The citizens of the town were going about their day, just as they had been when Annie had ridden through on her way to rescue a heartsick dragon's teddy bear.

The scene through the window, however, no longer resembled a fairy tale. The children weren't playing hopscotch or skip-the-stone today. In fact, they weren't playing together at all. Two boys wrestled on the cobblestones, using their fists to inflict as much damage as possible to each other's faces. One little girl sat by herself, crying quietly while a group of other girls stood nearby, whispering and laughing as they watched. The women who had chatted merrily as they carried water back and forth from the well now passed each other without a word, chins held high and haughty eyes averted.

It was nothing like the peaceful, happy place she remembered.

"The man rode through the village square just moments ago," the Lady said, "and left the ugliness you see in his wake. He did not speak to anyone. He did not need to. So strongly connected is he to the emotions of others that he has the ability to not just sense them, but actually influence them.

He uses this connection," she pointed one gnarled finger at the brawling children, "to seek out our darker feelings, the ones we keep hidden from the world. Then, he amplifies them, so that they become more a part of who we are.

For the creatures in the meadow, he chose self-doubt, that tiny part of them that holds its breath whenever they unfurl their wings, afraid that this time, they will not rise. He used that fear, usually buried deep, to overcome the confidence born of a lifetime of flight.

With Clarence, he awakened instincts that the poor creature had spent years learning to control. What you saw in the town hall was who Clarence is…"

Annie opened her mouth to argue.

"Or rather," the Lady amended, "it could have been. Born a predator, Clarence made different choices about who he wanted to be, nurturing his desire to protect others instead. He really is rather remarkable; he has to work so much harder to be kind than most of us do."

She brushed her hand against the window as if clearing frost from the glass, and the scene vanished.

"Be a dear and put some more wood on that fire," the Lady said, sitting back down in her rocking chair.

Annie took an armful of logs from the basket beside the stove. She opened the door and stuffed them into the heart of the blaze. The flames roared to life, filling the room with light and warmth.

Annie sat down again, leaning forward to hold her hands in front of the fire.

"One thing I don't get," she said, "is how the man came to life in the first place. Grimsley says it's because of me?"

The Lady looked thoughtful.

"The man, or some version of him at any rate, has always been here," she said.

Annie sat up hopefully. Maybe this wasn't her fault after all. But that hope was dashed with the Lady's next words.

"However, your recent arrival is indeed responsible for his current incarnation. Like everything else in Bibylonia, he is shaped by your thoughts and your imagination. As you change, so does this world we inhabit. Something you brought with you from your own world allowed the man to take this form."

"But…."

The Lady interrupted her gently. "All of the negative emotions John Doe chooses to manipulate; anger, hatred, jealousy, they all stem from the same thing – fear. Can you not think of any way you could have brought fear with you?"

She could.

"Yes," she said, so quietly it was almost a whisper.

"The magic of this place is unpredictable," the Lady said, "as you learned when you discovered Captain Downing's new home, born of an afternoon's musings. The fear that you carry in your own heart was the catalyst that brought self-awareness to the man, and shaped what kind of creature he would be."

"I didn't know," Annie said miserably. "I just wanted to…to be somewhere I didn't have to feel like that anymore."

The Lady's expression was kind.

"I know that, child. We made the choice to bring you here knowing there was risk. Human emotion is one of the most powerful forces in the world, and also one of the most dangerous."

Her gaze wandered to the walls where the windows were. "What's done is done. Now we must deal with what is to come."

"He wants out," Annie said quickly. "Into my world, I mean. He wanted me to give him my key."

The Lady's expression did not change. Annie got the feeling not much happened in Bibylonia that took her by surprise.

"What would happen if he did get out?" she asked. "I mean, I'm just a kid at home, not a hero. He wouldn't be able to do the same things there that he can do here either, right?"

"Should the man escape the boundaries of Bibylonia, your world would face the same danger as ours. People do not truly change, Annie," the Lady said. "They are who they are, wherever they are. For example, the girl who wakes every day in the garden is the same girl who goes to sleep in your bedroom each night."

Annie shook her head but didn't argue. That was something the Lady couldn't possibly understand; how different she was here; how much easier it was to be the person she wanted to be. Anyway, she had her answer. If John Doe got out, he would do the same thing he was doing here.

Which was what, exactly?

She tried to imagine the ways that the man could use his gift in her world. She thought of Clarence, and how a creature she knew to be gentle and kind had suddenly become incredibly dangerous. Still, how much damage could he do if he was using his power on regular people instead of giant cobras that could kill everything in the room in a matter of minutes?

Suddenly, she remembered something her father had told her when they were watching a movie about World War Two. "Governments don't go to war, Annie," he had said. "People do." Hitler had been just a "regular" person.

"So," she said slowly, "If he got out, he could use his power to start a war?"

The Lady inclined her head. "That is one possibility. It would be simple enough for him to escalate those feelings of competitiveness that so often exist between people in power."

"Why would anyone want to do something like that?" she asked, horrified.

"As to that, I cannot say for certain. I suspect that his motives are actually quite simple. It is what he excels at and being good at something is always satisfying."

It made a strange kind of sense to Annie. After all, being in Bibylonia was satisfying to her, not just because of the adventures, but because puzzling through a problem and coming up with the solution was something she did well. Besides, the man himself had told her something similar - that doing these things was what made him happy.

A thought occurred to Annie. "If I had just kept reading those stupid princess stories we wouldn't be in this mess," she said, miserably. "The bad guys in those are never very smart, so they're easy to beat. All you need is a prince with a sword or a little bit of magic."

The Lady laughed.

"Yes, child, had your imaginings remained simpler, the villain you conjured might be more easily dispatched. However, had you not opened your mind to a wider world, this place might not even exist at all. We might still be rabbits and squirrels, scampering through the meadow."

The Lady rose from her chair. As she did, the little blue door swung open again. Annie understood that it was time for her to go.

She got up and headed for the door. As she reached forward to grasp the handle, the old woman's fingers closed over her outstretched hand.

"All is not lost, Anneliese. The man is dangerous, but he has no power to force people to his will."

"But...what about what happened to Clarence?" Annie stammered.

"All creatures have the ability to wage war against the darkest parts of themselves and win. But this battle is too difficult for most to bear. It is far easier to give in, especially when something is forcing those feelings to the forefront."

"Clarence would never just give in," Annie protested. "He's a police officer, and...and, he's my friend."

The Lady squeezed her hand tightly. "Of course he is. Otherwise, he certainly would have killed you. There was nothing to stop him except Clarence himself."

She thought about that. It was true that the other animals had found it almost impossible to hold him down. He probably could have reached her before any of them were able to do anything about it. But he hadn't. Some part of him had wanted to, but he hadn't.

She nodded to show that she understood, then stepped through the door. Grimsley and Marty stood exactly where she had left them, as if she had been gone only seconds.

Looking back at the Lady, she posed the question she had been most afraid of asking.

"Should I go home now?"

By go home, she meant go back to her own world and never return to Bibylonia. She knew the Lady would understand what she meant.

"Only you can make that decision, child. It is no one's place to guide your conscience except your own."

The Lady closed the door, which immediately disappeared, leaving Annie with more questions than when she had arrived.

CHAPTER 36
THE INTERVENTION

Annie woke on Saturday morning to a strangely quiet house. When she went downstairs, she found her mom and dad sitting on the sofa, and her little sister was nowhere in sight. That explained the lack of noise.

Her parents' heads turned as she came down the stairs. They were strangely synchronized, like the motorized characters on amusement park rides. Alarm bells sounded in Annie's brain.

"Where's Maisy?" she asked.

"She's down the street at the Robertsons' playing with Laura," her father replied.

At nine o'clock in the morning?

"Sit down, please," her mother said, her expression serious.

Annie sat in the space they had made between them, and immediately felt trapped.

"Annie," her mother continued, "your behavior lately has been really out of the ordinary. You hardly touch your food, and as far as I can tell you haven't picked up a book in weeks."

Annie hunched over, pulling her knees up to her chest and wrapping her arms around them.

"Whatever's going on with you, you don't seem to want to talk about it with us. So, your father and I have decided that we need some help."

Annie stared at her, uncomprehending.

"We're going to see your school counselor on Thursday," her father said gently. "It's her job to help kids work through their problems. Whatever's bothering you, I guarantee you she's dealt with it before."

Ms. Ward. They had scheduled an appointment with Ms. Ward, the one adult who actually knew something about why Annie had been so unhappy lately. Her panic was a living thing in her chest, pushing to get out. She jumped up like her seat was on fire.

"No way," she said flatly. "I'm not going."

Her parents gaped at her. Annie couldn't blame them for being shocked. She had always been the kid who did what she was told – at home, at school, pretty much everywhere. Unlike a lot of her classmates, she had never even been grounded.

"I said, I'm not going," she repeated. "And you can't make me."

And with that, she turned and ran up the stairs into her room, slamming the door behind her.

CHAPTER 37
THE LONGEST DAYS

Annie stayed in her room all weekend. Her parents came to the door every few hours, trying different tactics to get her to talk to them about what was wrong, but she turned to face the wall whenever they came in.

She was aware of the passage from day into night only by the dimming of the light spilling around the edges of her curtains. When the sky outside her window was completely dark, Annie heard her bedroom door creak open. She didn't move or give any other sign that she might be awake, hoping whoever it was would give up and leave. Instead, her mother crawled into her bed and curled up beside Annie in the dark. She lay there for a long time, never saying a word. Finally, she kissed Annie's cheek before getting up and leaving the room. After the door closed behind her, Annie reached up and touched her face, wiping away the tears her mother had left behind. That was the second time in as many days that her mother had cried. Because of her.

CHAPTER 38
THE EMPTY FOREST

Eventually Annie did fall asleep, overwhelmed by the emotional exhaustion of the day. After waking in her usual spot in the garden she was on her feet before Marty's tail had even started twitching. There had to be something she could do to fix things here, even if things were falling apart in the real world.

She needed to talk to the Lady. The Lady would know what to do.

The gate was rustier and creakier than it had been even the day before, and Annie struggled for several minutes to get the old iron key to turn in the lock. She didn't even wait for her clothes to settle into place after her transformation before she took off running. She wanted to see Grimsley first, if only to know that he was still safe.

But when she reached the edge of the forest where the Guardians had previously stood guard, they were nowhere to be seen. She gazed out into the fields surrounding the forest and found them deserted as well.

She decided to look for them. She set off down the path with Marty, feeling a little lost without the map to guide her. Even though it was the middle of the day, Bibylonia appeared to be deserted. The whole country looked like one of those towns that got preserved the way they were in the old West for tourists to visit.

When an hour or so had passed without seeing any signs of life, she gave up and turned back towards the forest. Maybe the Lady had sent them all into hiding. She pictured the entire population of Bibylonia safe in an underground bunker, while John Doe rode aimlessly up and down the countryside. Somehow, she had a feeling it wouldn't be that easy.

She craned her head in every direction as they walked, hoping to catch a glimpse of someone, anyone, who might be able to tell her where the rest of the world had gone. But even the animals seemed to have taken cover. It made Annie uneasy.

She had thought she remembered the way to the Lady's home, but try as she might, she couldn't find it. After riding past the same mossy boulder three times, she had to admit she was lost.

As soon as she realized this, she came to another, more disturbing realization. Not only did she not know how to get to the Lady's tree, she also had no idea how to get back to the garden. She was deeper in the forest than she had ever been before, and there were no landmarks to guide her.

She climbed down from Marty's back and sat down on a fallen log to collect her thoughts. Leaning back, she closed her eyes, intending to rest for a few minutes before continuing on. She wondered briefly what would happen if she fell asleep in Bibylonia, but she never got the chance to find out.

At the sound of Marty's guttural growl, she sat up abruptly, her heart pounding. She jumped up, looking around for the source of whatever had caused him to sound a warning.

It didn't take her long to spot the source of his agitation. She laughed out loud in spite of her ebbing panic and swatted the tiger on the back of the head.

"Seriously, ding-dong?" she scolded him. "All that noise over a squirrel?"

Annie was pretty sure it was the same black squirrel she kept seeing all over Bibylonia. She had seen it for the first time in this forest, so it probably lived here.

"Go on now," Annie told it, making shooing motions with her hands. "Get out of here, before my stupid cat tries to eat you."

It didn't move. It watched her with bright, intelligent eyes. Annie suddenly remembered where she was; this might not be an ordinary squirrel.

Annie crouched down. "Um, can I help you?" she asked.

It chittered bossily at her, which made Marty growl again. Annie shushed the tiger quickly and turned to the squirrel again.

It had moved while her back was turned, and now sat four or five feet down the path ahead of her. She stood up, moving slowly to avoid startling the animal. As soon as she began walking, however, it turned and scampered away from her.

"No!" Annie called out. "Come back – I won't hurt you."

The squirrel stopped, but when Annie took another few steps forward, it darted down the path again.

She started to run, not concerned anymore about scaring the squirrel. This time she meant to catch it. It might not be an actual person, but this was Bibylonia, and it was always possible that the squirrel could tell her where everyone else was. Unfortunately, it seemed to anticipate this and began to run when she did. Marty, seeing a game of chase-the squirrel in play, leapt forward with delight and took off down the path after it.

"Stupid cat!" Annie yelled, running as fast as she could, trying to keep him in sight as he bounded through the trees. The last thing she needed was to be lost in the middle of the forest, exhausted and without a ride home. "Get back here!"

Annie chased the tiger chasing the squirrel for a long time, until her ribs ached, and she couldn't catch her breath. Just when she thought she couldn't go another step, Marty skidded to a stop on the path ahead of her.

She slowed to a walk; fingers pressed hard against the stitch in her side. When she reached Marty, she smacked him on the shoulder.

"Thanks a lot, furball."

As she stepped around the tiger to see what had caused him to abandon the chase, she was surprised to see the squirrel sitting directly in front of him. It shifted its eyes to Annie briefly before scampering up the nearest tree and out of sight.

"That's one thing that's the same in both worlds," Annie muttered. "Squirrels are crazy."

Sighing heavily, she sat down in the middle of the path next to Marty. Leaning against his back, she looked around again for any sign of something familiar. This time, she found it.

The gate that led into Annie's garden stood just over the rise of a nearby hill. Annie turned quickly back towards the squirrel that had guided her home, but it was nowhere in sight.

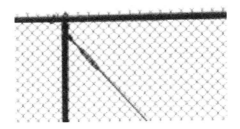

CHAPTER 39
ESCAPE

Jay arrived in homeroom with the bell the following morning, so she didn't get to talk to him until recess. Ever since the incident on the bus they had continued to read together rather than run around like they usually would. It wasn't like they had ever discussed it; they just fell into the habit the same way they had started sitting as close as possible to the teachers in the cafeteria.

Today the book Jay had brought was too disgusting for even Annie – something about parasites that live in people's intestines. With color pictures. Jay put the book down on the bench, trying unsuccessfully to hide his disappointment.

"Well, if we're not going to read my book," he complained, "maybe you could tell me another story about Bibylonia?"

"No, I couldn't," she snapped at him, irritably.

Jay's eyes widened and he looked away, towards the kids playing kickball on the soccer field. Annie immediately felt terrible. She could count on one hand the number of times either of them had spoken sharply to the other in the whole time they'd been friends. It wasn't Jay's fault that Bibylonia was no longer an enjoyable subject for her.

She had just opened her mouth to apologize when she was distracted by the sight of all four of the recess monitors running by. That was something you didn't see every day. Annie watched in amazement as the teachers closed in on two boys in the throes of a full-on fistfight on top of the climbing structure. Even more amazing was who it was; Ray and Owen had been best friends since kindergarten.

Their own almost-argument forgotten, Annie and Jay jumped up and ran towards the commotion, along with every other kid on the playground. The teachers were shouting up at the boys to stop fighting right now, circling the climbing structure so they could catch them if they fell. But the boys were intent on their struggle and didn't even seem to realize that they had an audience.

Annie wasn't sure what made her look away from the fight. Maybe it was the similarity to the scene in Aesoppla she had seen through the window in the Lady's tree, or maybe it was just the now ingrained habit of checking for the location of the twins. Whatever it was, after a few minutes she tore her eyes from the play structure to scan the rest of the playground.

John Doe stood behind the chain link fence, the unicorn nosing through the weeds at his feet. He smiled and gave her a friendly little wave.

I'm dreaming, Annie thought. I'm so tired I've fallen asleep on my feet. She was still trying to convince herself when she felt someone tugging at her sleeve.

"Hey, you're missing the good stuff," Jay said insistently. "They're actually hanging upside down now and they're still fighting. Come on, what are you…"

Jay stopped midsentence, his hand suddenly limp against her arm.

"What is that?" he whispered.

Annie looked at him sharply. His eyes were trained on John Doe, now disappearing into the woods.

Jay's fingers worked at the fabric of her jacket as he watched him go. "There was something…something not quite…was that a unicorn?" he asked weakly.

And with that, Annie knew. She wasn't asleep. She was in her own world, and the man was here.

CHAPTER 40
THE PLAN

Annie sat down on the ground with a thump. She wasn't sure her legs would carry her back to the bench where they had been reading in blissful ignorance only moments ago. Jay sat with her, both ignoring the noise of the fight still happening just a few feet away.

"Are you okay?" Jay asked tentatively.

Annie began to cry, deep, racking sobs that made it hard to catch her breath. She cried for a long time, until her head hurt and her eyes burned and the skin on her face felt tight and sore. It was the first time in her life she had cried like that in front of anyone but her parents.

Jay made no effort to comfort her. With the instincts that only best friends have about each other, he seemed to understand that she needed to get it out of her system before she could talk at all. He sat in sympathetic silence, waiting for her to be ready.

When Annie finally felt capable of speech again, she knew it was time to tell Jay the truth about Bibylonia. She told him everything. She couldn't meet his eyes when she explained about the man, but she didn't leave anything out. Jay deserved to know just how much trouble they were in.

She could see that he was skeptical at first. She couldn't blame him; it was a crazy story. She hadn't believed it at first either. She just had to hope that after so many years of friendship, he would know that she always told him the truth. Even if this time it had taken her a while to get around to it.

Jay didn't immediately respond when she finished talking. He sat frowning at his feet, the way he did when puzzling over a particularly difficult math problem.

Finally, he looked up at her.

"I believe you," he said. "I think I kind of have to. Not even you could make up something that complicated and insane."

The tightness in Annie's chest eased just enough for her to laugh.

"Actually, that's pretty much the problem. I did make up something that complicated and insane. I just didn't mean to."

As they sat there, forgotten by the teachers who had finally managed to drag the fighters off the play structure, Annie found herself wishing she had told Jay the truth weeks ago. Having him to talk to made everything seem a little more manageable, somehow.

"We have to go," Jay said decisively, standing up and brushing dirt off the seat of his pants.

"Go?" Annie looked at him blankly.

"We have to get help. This isn't something we can handle on our own."

"So where are we supposed to go for help?" Annie asked, bewildered.

"Bibylonia, of course." Jay looked at her as if this were obvious.

She stared at him. "How do you think we're going to do that? It's the middle of the day! Anyway," she said, "I'm not even sure I could bring you with me. Grimsley said the only thing I can bring into Bibylonia from this world is Marty."

"I don't think the old rules apply anymore," he said thoughtfully. "If the man is here, that means that he had to get past all the usual stuff that's supposed to keep people from moving back and forth between places."

Once she realized Jay was serious, Annie started thinking that it might actually be possible. He was right – the man had to have gotten through the gate to get here, so maybe she could take someone in the other direction. Grimsley had told her she could learn to cross over when she was awake, but she had no idea how to do it. So, for this to work, they had to be together, and asleep. Definitely not an easy thing to arrange.

It might have been impossible, had they not been the two smartest kids in the sixth grade. As it was, it took them only a few minutes to come up with a plan that just might work.

CHAPTER 41
TO SLEEP, TO DREAM

"I don't know if I can do this," Jay said anxiously.

They stood facing each other on the deserted playground, about twenty feet apart.

"It was your idea!" Annie reminded him.

"I know it was," he whined. "But I still don't know if I can do it."

Annie sighed. They didn't have a whole lot of time.

"Look," she said firmly, "let's just do it, before you have a chance to freak out. One, two, three, GO!"

They ran towards each other as fast as they could. Annie couldn't help but laugh when she saw that Jay was running with his eyes closed. As they got closer and she actually thought about what they were about to do, however, it was all she could do to keep from closing her own.

CRUNCH.

Just as they had intended, their heads collided with a sound like a dropped watermelon. They fell backwards, clutching their faces in agony. After a few minutes, they both sat up, still groaning, and crawled towards each other to inspect the damage. Annie could see the beginnings of a nasty lump on Jay's forehead, just above his left eyebrow. Judging by her own throbbing temple, she had a similar injury.

Step one of Operation Get to Bibylonia was complete.

They stumbled down the hallway, holding onto each other for balance. They did not need to convince the nurse that they needed to lie down. She took one look and hurried them off to a storage room at the back of her office, where she set up two cots before leaving to deal with the injuries from the recess brawl.

"Sweet," Jay groaned. "We didn't even have to use our cover stories."

They had spent the walk from the playground coming up with complicated explanations for why the nurse wouldn't be able to reach their parents so they wouldn't get carted home before they could implement the rest of the plan.

The hardest part, strangely enough, was actually going to sleep. Annie wasn't used to sleeping anywhere but her own room. Not only that, they had decided that to maximize their chances of arriving in Bibylonia together, they needed to make sure they were touching each other when they fell asleep. So, they had pushed their cots together, and Annie had tied her right hand to Jay's left with the drawstring from her jacket. She really hoped the nurse didn't walk back in while they were sleeping. She didn't want to try to explain that.

"Okay, now remember," Jay whispered, "as you're falling asleep, you need to concentrate on both of us arriving together in Bibylonia. You're the one who knows how to get there, so just focus on me being with you when you arrive. If you…"

"Jay," Annie said through gritted teeth, "if you explain this to me one more time, I'm going to conk you over the head with a stapler and go by myself."

"Okay. Sheesh."

As exhausted as she was, sleep seemed to be just out of Annie's reach. Every time she began to drift off, some noise in the hallway beyond would startle her awake and she would have to start all over again.

Glancing over at Jay, she saw that he was in the same boat. His eyes were closed, but his face was scrunched up in concentration. The sight of his furrowed forehead and wrinkled nose made Annie smile. She was so grateful that she didn't have to do this alone.

With that comforting thought, she closed her eyes, still facing her friend, and fell asleep.

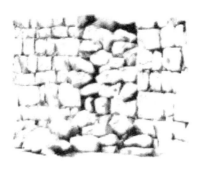

CHAPTER 42
THE FALLEN WALL

They woke up together in the garden, momentarily jubilant at their success. It took some work to untie the knots holding their hands together. Once they were free Annie rolled off the now completely brown moss onto the cobblestoned path.

"This isn't the way I imagined this place based on the way you described it." Jay said sadly.

There wasn't a single flower left. Every bit of the garden was withered and brown, like her own garden at home in the dead of winter. The only thing that was still alive was the ivy, which had finally overwhelmed the crumbling garden walls. The huge grey stones that had framed the gate lay scattered on the ground, completely covered with twisted vines the size of Annie's arm. The gaping holes where the stones had been were wide enough, Annie realized with a sick feeling in her stomach, to ride a horse through. The lingering smell of rotten garbage hung in the air.

The gate itself still stood, a mocking reminder that she hadn't managed to do the one thing she had been asked to do from her first arrival – keep anything from coming through.

The wooden door that brought her home after an adventure stood ajar, even though she knew she had closed it behind her the night before. She walked over and pushed it open.

On the other side, she saw her own bedroom. Her parents and Maisy had been walking out the door that morning as she sprinted for the bus, so at least she knew they hadn't been home when the man came through. She hoped Marty had hidden under the bed.

Speaking of which…

She looked around to see if he had somehow made the journey to

Bibylonia with them, even though Annie hadn't been at home when she fell asleep. But the cat was nowhere to be seen.

A sudden rustling froze Annie in her tracks. She held her finger to her lips to warn Jay to stay quiet, and they waited.

The sound came again, like footsteps on dry leaves. It was coming from the grotto in the center of the garden. Suddenly hopeful, she grabbed Jay's hand, and together they ran down the path. Ducking under the tangle of dead branches that had once been covered with pink flowers, they entered the clearing. Just as Annie had suspected, there was someone there, pacing back and forth across the dirt floor.

Grimsley.

Annie nearly tripped over her own feet in her haste to get to her friend. She locked her arms around the rabbit's neck and hugged him as hard as she could.

"Miss Annie," he croaked feebly after a few moments. "I am glad to see you, but you are making it hard for me to breathe."

"Sorry," she said sheepishly, letting go. "I'm just so glad you're safe."

Grimsley looked down at his feet.

"No one is safe, Miss Annie," he said. "Not anymore."

"I know," she said quietly, taking his paws in her hands. "We saw him, Grim. At my school."

Jay made a soft noise of astonishment behind her.

He was standing where Annie had left him, gaping at Grimsley. Annie supposed it probably wasn't often that you met a talking rabbit that you had previously thought was a fictional character.

"I always wondered how the two of you would get along," she said, smiling. "Grim, this is my friend Jay. Jay, this is…"

"Grimsley," he said weakly. "Yeah, I figured that out. Nice to meet you."

He stepped forward and held out his hand.

"I've heard a lot about you," he continued. "I just didn't know you were real until today."

"Grim," Annie said quickly. "I came last night to find the Lady, but I got lost trying to get to her tree. Can you guide us there?"

Grimsley shook his head. "The Lady is gone, Miss Annie. No amount of knocking will make the door appear. I have worn my own knuckles raw trying."

"Gone?" Annie echoed, horrified. "But, she's the leader of the Guardians! Aren't you guys supposed to be here to protect the gate?"

"The rest of the Guardians are also gone," he said sadly. "Where, I do not know. I was scheduled for guard duty yesterday at dawn. When I arrived, the forest was empty. I went to the Lady's tree, but when I could not find her either, I set out into Bibylonia to search. I looked all day and into the night. When I returned, the walls were down and the door to your world stood open."

Annie remembered how quiet the forest had been when she had arrived, devoid of life except for a single squirrel.

"There has to be someone else who can help us," Annie insisted. She was trying not to panic; they had miraculously managed to get here and now the one person Annie had counted on to know what to do could not be found.

"Wait a minute," she said, remembering something. "What about the queen?"

It seemed like years ago that they had walked along the path for the first time, getting to know each other while Grimsley shared stories about the citizens of Bibylonia. Although Annie had never even seen Queen Merriweather, she remembered the confident, capable girl Grimsley had described and felt a sudden surge of hope.

So, they set off together for the palace. Annie opened the gate with her key even though the walls were missing. She didn't want to walk in John Doe's footsteps. Grimsley had to hold Jay back from going to Annie's rescue when the wind engulfed her on the other side, and it was a good ten minutes before he stopped twisting his head as they walked to stare at her transformation.

The palace was only a short distance from the Village of Everlasting Snow, so Annie had passed it several times before. Usually it was bustling with activity; carriages passing through the gates, knights training on the wide green, and children flying kites from the hillside. Today, however, it was ominously quiet, like everywhere else they had passed along the way.

Annie rapped sharply on the gate. There was no response. She looked around for something that would make a louder noise and spotted a small brass bell hanging from the gatepost on a red velvet cord. She reached up and gave it a tug.

All three of them dropped to the ground at once, hands over their ears to block the deafening gong reverberating from the tiny bell. Annie was pretty sure she could have heard it from her garden. If anyone was inside the castle, they would know someone was here.

No one came. Jay thought he saw someone twitch a curtain aside in a tower window, but when the others turned to look there was nothing there. After waiting for a very long time, they finally had to face the fact that they were on their own.

They sat down to rest and brainstorm about what to do next. Jay, who had never been in Bibylonia before, was less bothered by the total absence of life they had encountered along the way. He had asked Grimsley for the map almost immediately after they sat down, and was now poring over it, fascinated. Meanwhile, Annie and Grimsley were racking their brains for anyone who might be able to help them fight John Doe.

"What about Harold?" Grimsley suggested.

"I'm not sure he's tough enough," Annie said. "He couldn't even stand up to that brat of a prince, remember?"

"You have a point," he agreed. "Captain Downing?"

"No, I went through Downingsburg last night. It's just as empty as everywhere else. Anyway, I'm not sure even he's a match for the man."

Grimsley sighed. "I fear that no one is, Miss Annie. With the Lady gone, I don't believe there is anyone in Bibylonia who could issue a summons to John Doe and win the day."

"Issue a what?" Jay asked.

"It means to challenge someone to something," Annie said, pleased to know something Jay didn't, for once. "Like a race, or a fight."

Grimsley nodded. "Exactly so. To issue a summons in Bibylonia is to challenge an adversary to a formal competition. It takes place in public, so that there can be no question of fairness. At the conclusion, one of the opponents is declared the winner by a panel of judges, and they both must abide by that ruling."

"So, what happens to the loser?" Jay asked.

"Whatever has been agreed upon," Grimsley replied. "The challenger sets the place and time, and the defender gets to name the penalty for losing."

That didn't sound good. "Can that penalty be anything?" Annie asked.

"Short of death, which our laws do not permit, yes."

Okay, so at least if John Doe was summoned, he wouldn't be able to kill anyone. She had thought of another potential problem, however.

"What about the fact that he's not even in Bibylonia anymore, Grim? How would someone be able to do this summoning thing?"

Grimsley frowned.

"In theory, it should not matter. Though he is not physically here, he is a citizen of Bibylonia, and bound by our laws. None may refuse to accept a summons. That is why the person who is summoned gets to determine what the stakes will be."

Annie had a moment to be glad that she had read so many fantasy novels over the years that took their cues from medieval history, where the rules for conflict and duels had been so well-defined.

Grimsley stood, brushing grass from the tops of his boots and reaching down to pull Annie to her feet.

"It makes no difference whether he can be summoned or not," he went on, "when there is no one who could stand against him. I hesitate to say it aloud, but I'm not sure even the Lady..."

"I'll do it," Annie said quietly.

She looked over at Jay and saw in his expression the same grim determination that she felt. There was no one left. No one but them. And the man had to be stopped.

CHAPTER 43
THE SCROLL

It took several minutes to calm Grimsley down after Annie announced her intention to issue a summons to John Doe. Once he could form words again, he immediately started trying to talk her out of it. First, he explained why she had absolutely no chance of winning. When she didn't back down, he claimed ignorance of how the process worked, that there was no way that he could guide them through the formal language that was required.

Annie noticed something strange about Grimsley's behavior as he made this declaration. He held his body at an odd angle, tucking his right foot behind his left. It looked very uncomfortable, and she couldn't imagine why he would choose to stand that way. She suddenly remembered the scroll that Grimsley had read from when welcoming her to Bibylonia. There had been a lot of writing on that scroll, quite a bit more than the little section he had read out loud. It had trailed the ground, rolling over the top of the boot he had removed to retrieve it. His right boot.

She sat abruptly down on the ground, plastering a defeated look on her face. Jay gaped at her disbelievingly. Grimsley stooped in front of her, reaching down to touch her shoulder. Her arms shot out and she pulled hard at his knees, knocking him onto his back in the grass.

Hurriedly she began to tug at his right boot. His eyes widened as he realized what she was trying to do, and he clung desperately to the boot to keep it on.

But he was fighting a losing battle. Unbalanced by the fall, he was no match for Annie's determination to get her hands on what she needed. She gave a mighty tug and the boot came free, the odd collection of items Grimsley carried with him everywhere tumbling out onto the ground.

Including the scroll.

Snatching it up, she jumped to her feet and shook it out, reading as quickly as she could. Sure enough, near the bottom of the yellowing paper was a small section labeled, "To Issue a Summons." She scanned through it quickly, absorbing what she had to do.

"I'm sorry, Grim," she told the miserable rabbit, reaching down to help him to his feet. "I have to do this. I know I don't have much of a chance, but we don't have any other options."

She hugged him tightly, trying not to cry. "You don't have to watch if you don't want to."

He put his trembling arms around her neck, his ears drooping low. "I will not leave you," he whispered.

CHAPTER 44
THE SUMMONS

The language required for the summons was simple, and short enough that Annie only needed to glance at it twice before she began. When she had finished speaking, she handed the scroll back to Grimsley and they settled in to wait.

They didn't have to wait for long. Only a few minutes had passed when John Doe rode into view, looking just as ordinary and just as wrong as ever. Annie folded her arms across her chest as she watched him approach, trying not to look as terrified as she felt.

He climbed down from the unicorn's back and ambled lazily towards them. Instinctively, they moved closer together.

"You understand that I'm not obligated to choose terms that will allow you to save your little world?" he addressed Annie with a smile. "You could summon me until the end of days, and I could just keep choosing to fight for who wears a hat on Fridays, or whether your friend there gets to keep his boots."

He nodded amiably at Grimsley, who whimpered.

The idea that the man could so easily stop her from doing what had to be done was infuriating. But Grimsley had told her there was no way around it – the defender got to set the stakes. In order to have a chance at protecting her friends and family, she had to convince him to fight on her terms. And she thought she already knew how to make that happen.

"Seems kind of boring to me," she said, flippantly. "I wouldn't have bothered to summon you if I'd known you were going to waste my time."

His eyes narrowed for a moment. Then his face cleared, and he chuckled.

"Oh, come now. Such an obvious attempt at manipulation? Really, I would have thought better of you."

Annie didn't respond immediately. She was watching the man. No matter what he said, she could see that her words had affected him. A dark red flush crept slowly up his neck, and he was rocking back and forth on the balls of his feet.

"Okay, whatever, then," she said, with an impatient sigh, rolling her eyes in the way that so irritated her mother. "Just pick already. If we're going to fight over something stupid, I want to go ahead and get it over with."

She arranged her features in a bored expression and idly twisted a lock of her long hair around one finger. She pretended not to notice that Grimsley and Jay were staring at her as if she had gone insane.

The man's friendly smile didn't waver, but Annie saw a muscle jumping at his temple that hadn't been there before.

"Very well, my dear," he said stiffly. "You wish to fight over something that matters. Shall we make the stakes as high as possible?"

Annie almost panicked then, but reminded herself that the man couldn't kill her, even if he won. Surely anything else she could deal with.

"If you defeat me," he declared, "I will willingly return to the Grey Plains and never again venture beyond its borders."

Annie's heart beat faster; it was exactly what she had been hoping for.

"If I am victorious, however," he continued, "I will return to your world for the rest of my days. You will remain in Bibylonia for the rest of yours."

Annie felt the bottom drop out of her stomach. Sure, there had been times she had desperately wished that she lived in Bibylonia, but to never go home, never see her family again? Those stakes were just too high.

On the other hand, if she refused, there was nothing to prevent him from walking back through that little wooden door into her house, where her family would soon return. The only way to protect them was to send him back where he belonged.

"Agreed,"she said. "We meet in two hours, in World's Beginning/World's End."

"How…appropriate." He bowed. "Until then."

He climbed back onto his unicorn's back and was gone.

"How did you know," Jay asked quietly, "what to say to make him agree to be banished if you win?"

"I'm not exactly sure. I just thought fighting over something that didn't matter to me wouldn't be any fun for him. Having power over other people is the only thing that makes him happy."

She reached inside her collar, closing her fingers over the rusty key. "And, I got so angry when I thought he might be able to weasel out of a fight that I guess I forgot to be afraid for a while. He didn't like that, so he gave me something to be afraid of. I think he even knew it was what I wanted him to do, but he just couldn't help himself."

Jay shook his head. "Hey, Grimsley," he asked, "When was the last time someone issued a summons? I figure it has to have happened before, or you wouldn't have rules written down for it."

"Yes, it has happened before, Mr. Jay, but only once. It is not something we speak of."

Grimsley cast a nervous, sideways glance at Annie.

Annie sighed. She was never going to get to hear that story.

CHAPTER 45
THE LONG WALK

They went back to the garden to wait. Even though it wasn't protected anymore, it was still her garden, and it felt safer than anywhere else in Bibylonia right now.

As Grimsley had explained while they were walking, there weren't really any rules for the contest except the no killing part. So, there wasn't much they could do to plan. Instead, they spent the time talking and sharing stories, anything to take their minds off what was coming.

"Hey, Grim," Annie had just thought of something. "Aren't we supposed to have witnesses to this fight? We haven't seen anyone all day."

"The Queen will have been alerted by the summons," Grimsley told her. "She will assemble the witnesses and the panel of judges from wherever they are hiding."

"Oh. Okay." It didn't seem like there was much they could do except wait for it to be time.

"Time" happened alarmingly quickly. It felt like they had just returned to the garden when suddenly they had to go. Even though she knew it was pointless, Annie locked the gate behind her as they left, feeling it shudder loosely in its frame. She stepped onto the path and waited for the wind.

When the dust at her feet finally settled, Annie knew immediately that something about this transformation had been different, even without Grimsley's gasp of surprise. She looked down at her clothes. Instead of the leggings she usually wore in Bibylonia, the forest had provided a pair of soft brown leather pants with matching knee-high boots. She still had her green tunic, but over it was a second shirt, made of gleaming chain mail. Her drawstring pouch hung on a wide leather belt, studded with tiny silver rivets.

She carried no weapons, but otherwise she was dressed for war.

Jay looked hopefully down at his own clothes, which hadn't changed at all.

"Oh, well," he sighed. "I'm not sure leather pants would be that comfortable, anyway."

Annie tried to laugh, but the sound got stuck in her throat.

The forest was eerily still. When she finally did catch movement out of the corner of her eye, it startled her so badly that she jumped.

It was only that black squirrel again. It raced down the trunk of a nearby tree and stopped in front of them, surveying them for a moment through bright brown eyes. Then, it bounded down the path and disappeared.

As they walked, Annie patted her belt pouch to make sure it was still securely attached. She was counting on it to deliver what she needed to defend herself against John Doe.

She glanced over at Jay, who was craning his head in every direction so he wouldn't miss anything. Annie leaned into Grimsley's shoulder and whispered as quietly as she could into his ear.

"No matter what happens, Grim, I need you to do something for me."

"What, Miss Annie?" he whispered back.

"Make sure Jay gets home."

His eyes widened, but he nodded.

"I'm so sorry, Grim," she said. "For asking you to do this. For, you know, everything."

"I'm not giving up yet, Miss Annie," he took her hand and squeezed it. "You don't give up either."

CHAPTER 46
FACING OFF

When they arrived at the meadow, they found it completely unrecognizable. The soft, drifting grasses had been replaced with scrubby, uneven weeds and bare dirt. There were no flowers or fairies in sight. A chain link fence bordered the meadow on three sides, and a brightly colored climbing structure stood in its center.

In other words, it was an exact replica of the playground at Annie's school.

Everyone she had ever met in Bibylonia was there. Clarence, the clock-keeper and Mrs. Otter, her paws on the arms of Bob the mongoose's wheelchair. Will Sykes and the other wood elves. Captain Downing. Harold the dragon, with the teddy-bear-stealing prince in tow. Even the black squirrel sat cleaning its paws on top of one of the swing sets. The playground was crowded with people, animals, and everything in-between.

A girl Annie had never seen before was clambering down from the climbing structure. She wore a plain grey jumpsuit, like the ones workmen wore on TV. She had pulled her long black hair into a messy knot on the top of her head, and a pale, freckled face peeked out from underneath bright blue bangs.

Grimsley leaned in and whispered, "Queen Merriweather."

Once the queen was on the ground, Annie could see that she was small for her age, no taller than Annie herself. She walked with long strides, her arms swinging loosely. Her nose was pierced, and she was chewing an enormous wad of gum.

"Been hoping to meet you since you got here," she said, sticking out her hand. "Sorry it has to be like this, though."

She cracked her gum, loudly.

Annie took her hand and shook it, a little bewildered. Grimsley had told her the queen was unconventional, but she hadn't been expecting…well…a teenager.

Before Annie could say anything, the noise level around them suddenly rose sharply. Annie turned to see a group of trolls stumbling backward to make way for the cause of the commotion.

John Doe.

Unlike Annie, he wore his everyday clothes. His monstrous unicorn followed obediently behind him, and Annie saw several of the ice giants press their frosty hands to their faces to block the smell.

The crowd scattered towards the fences as the man crossed the playground. He whistled tunelessly as he walked, sending the fur on Grimsley's back up in a line. When he reached the spot where Annie and Merriweather stood, he nodded politely before extending his hand to the queen.

She looked at it, then back at his face, one eyebrow raised.

"Like I'm going to let you touch me," she said sarcastically. "Listen, the rules say I have to let this contest happen, but nowhere does it say I have to be polite to you."

Annie thought the man might get angry, but he smiled indulgently at the queen, as if she was a precocious child.

"Another brave spirit, I see. Hmm, I must wonder, however," he said thoughtfully, "why you yourself did not challenge me. Or perhaps your pet wise woman who lives in the woods? Instead, you hid from me, and your Lady is nowhere to be found. It took a child, and one not even of this world to raise her voice against me."

Secretly, Annie thought he had a point. Why hadn't the queen or the Lady issued the summons? They were in charge here, after all. Annie looked quickly at Merriweather to see how she would respond.

She laughed, but Annie thought it sounded a little too loud, a little too confident. She glanced down and noticed that the queen's hands were balled into fists at her sides, and they were shaking.

Merriweather was afraid. And trying very hard not to show it.

"I'm tired of this conversation already," she said, waving one hand dismissively and turning away from him.

John Doe took a polite step backwards, a satisfied smile on his face.

Queen Merriweather raised both arms above her head to get the crowd's attention.

"Okay, everybody knows why we're here. And you all know the rules. But I've got to spell them out anyway, so pay attention."

She reached into the pocket of her jumpsuit and pulled out a tissue. After spitting the giant wad of gum into it, she tucked it back into her pocket and continued.

"Right. So, first of all, no killing each other." She glared fiercely at the man. "So, obviously, no lethal weapons allowed."

She jerked her head at a group of teenage girls, and two of them stepped forward. They wore steel-toed boots, ripped jeans, leather jackets, and swords. One of them slouched over to Annie, while the other approached John Doe. Annie felt strong hands lifting up her hair and patting down her clothes.

"No outside help, either. The judges," she pointed to a group of pirates standing near the swings, "will be watching to make sure that no one interferes. The contest is over when one of you falls. Whoever is left standing is the winner.

Next," she continued, "the terms have been established. If John Doe loses, he goes home to the Grey Plains, and he never comes back."

Anxious whispers spread through the gathered crowd. Annie was pretty sure she heard Clarence hiss.

"If Annie loses, he will return to her world, and she will remain here with us for the rest of her life."

This time, the crowd was so quiet that Annie could almost hear her own heartbeat.

"Do you both agree to these terms?" she asked.

They nodded.

"Well, that's it, then," she said. "Time to rock and roll."

She stepped close to Annie, casting another baleful glare at the man as she did. She grabbed Annie's hands and held them tightly.

"Listen, kid," she whispered fiercely, "you can do this. Remember who you are. No matter how scared you might be right now, you're still a hero."

She gave Annie's hands one final squeeze before clambering back up to the top of the climbing structure to wait for the contest to start.

Annie turned to Jay and Grimsley and found that she didn't have any words that were big enough to tell them how she felt. Instead, she hugged them both so tightly that she thought she heard one of Jay's ribs crack. Then Merriweather's guards were there again, to lead her friends away. And then it was time to begin.

CHAPTER 47
THE ONLY WEAPON SHE EVER NEEDED

Annie and John Doe faced each other in the center of the playground like gunslingers in the old West. From somewhere near the climbing structure a trumpet sounded, signaling the beginning of the contest. Annie glanced over and saw Jay and Grimsley sitting on either side of Merriweather, their faces apprehensive and fearful. The queen still wore that look of sneering confidence that Annie was pretty sure was just for show. Still, she appreciated that anyone was willing to say out loud that they thought there was a chance she could win.

Annie looked quickly back at the man, suddenly aware that she was staring off in the opposite direction from her opponent when the battle had already begun. But he hadn't moved; he stood with his hands in his pockets, his face relaxed. If he was planning to attack anytime soon, it didn't show.

Annie wondered what form that attack would take when it did come. She knew that John Doe's talent lay in bringing out the parts of people they usually tried to push down. With Clarence it had been his predatory instincts. What would it be for her?

Annie began to feel even more uneasy. She looked up at Jay, hoping for some kind of reassurance. His face was pale with fear, making the bruise across his cheek stand out starkly. She winced, remembering the horrible sound he had made when he landed in the dirt after being pushed from his swing. She had been right there, and what had she done to stop it? Nothing.

That hadn't been the only time she had let something like that happen, either. She could think of any number of times she had witnessed other kids getting harassed by the twins before they had turned their attention to Jay, and then subsequently to her. She had known at the time that someone needed to do something about it, but she hadn't wanted to risk drawing the twins' focus herself. So, she had simply looked away, and hoped that someone else would intervene.

Just like she always did, an ugly little voice whispered in her head.

What did that mean? It wasn't like she had a history of standing by and doing nothing before the twins came along. Okay, so there had been that one boy in her first-grade class who had transferred to their school in the middle of the year, which wasn't easy even if you were a regular kid. Stewart wasn't. He had ghost-white skin, thin, wispy hair and his face was spotted with blemishes that made him look older than he was. He never smiled. Annie hadn't picked on him like some of the other kids had, but she didn't go out of her way to stop them, either. She had been relieved when he hadn't shown up the following year.

She could have done something to protect Stewart, just like she could have stood up to the twins. But she had been too afraid to do the right thing. She was a coward. She always had been. She didn't deserve to be a hero.

Suddenly, she felt a sharp pain in her chest, and her eyes flew open. She hadn't even realized she had closed them. Reaching inside her tunic, she found the rusty key to her garden gate that had been digging into her skin, probably because she was doubled over, her head nearly touching her knees.

She straightened up, tucking it back inside her clothes. For a moment she completely forgot where she was. Then she heard the man's merry, delighted laugh, and she realized what had happened. John Doe's first assault had come without her even knowing she had been attacked. She thought about what the queen had said, that the contest would be over when the first person fell. She had almost lost it all in the first few seconds.

Looking around at the crowd, she saw that she hadn't been the only one affected. Clarence was thrashing around on the ground, hissing wildly. Mrs. Otter lay curled in a ball, weeping quietly. Several of the Guardians were in the throes of a brutal fistfight with the ice giants.

Annie turned towards the climbing structure. The queen and Grimsley had climbed or fallen to the bottom and sat huddled underneath it, their eyes wide with terror. Jay still sat at the top, staring down at the crowd with arrogant superiority. It was this more than anything else that spurred Annie into action. That wasn't an expression she had ever seen on Jay's face before, and she didn't want to ever see it again.

She untied the drawstring of her pouch with trembling hands, praying she'd be able to figure out how to use whatever she pulled out of it before things got any worse. She reached in and found...

Nothing. It was completely empty.

Annie felt the beginnings of real panic now. This had been her only chance for a weapon against the man's gift. The armor she was wearing was proof that the magic of the forest was still working. She had a problem that needed a solution, so the pouch should be offering up whatever tools she needed to solve it.

Annie stared out into the crowd and saw that the situation there was deteriorating. At this point, even if the man wasn't able to bring her down to officially win the contest, he would end up killing everyone in Bibylonia. Which, Annie thought, was probably his plan all along. He knew how much this place and its inhabitants meant to her. He had probably figured out that no matter how much she cared about her family, she couldn't stand by and let Grimsley and the others die either.

As Annie watched, her friends became unrecognizable as the uglier parts of their personalities took over. She thought about the memories that had almost overwhelmed her during the man's attack. All of them had been about times when she had stood by when other people needed her help. John Doe had reminded her that she might be brave in Bibylonia, but in her own life she was a coward.

Well, it was easier to be brave here, she thought, where she had magical tools to help her. But there was something about that argument, Annie realized, that didn't quite make sense. She had stopped a rampaging dragon with a dictionary and saved a whole town with a jar of peanut butter. Those weren't magical objects; they were ordinary, everyday things. The only thing special about them was how she had used them.

She thought about something the Lady had told her. "People do not truly change, Annie. They are who they are, wherever they are."

And suddenly she knew why the pouch was empty. She didn't need anything the pouch could provide. The only weapon she needed was…

"Me," she said out loud. And she took two steps forward.

John Doe's smile faltered. He had clearly expected her to remain under his spell like the others.

She lifted one hand and pointed at him.

"Fight me," she said. "Leave them out of it."

His smile widened again.

"Oh, my dear girl," he said sweetly. "Haven't you read enough books to know that the villain never plays fair?"

He waved lazily towards the crowd, and the noise level immediately escalated as the fighting became more frantic. Never taking his eyes from Annie, he began to walk slowly towards her.

Annie held her ground. She was still terrified, but she was done running away.

A grey blur suddenly appeared in Annie's peripheral vision, which quickly resolved into a figure standing between her and John Doe.

Grimsley.

His legs were shaking as badly as Annie had ever seen them, but the arrow aimed at John Doe's heart was perfectly steady.

"Grim, what are you doing?" she cried. "You can't interfere with the contest."

She ran forward and took him by the arm, gently lowering his bow. His face was wild, his lips pulled back from his teeth in a snarl, and he jumped when she touched him. He was almost insensible with fear, but he had still put himself between her and danger.

Annie walked him to the climbing structure and helped him back inside.

"Stay here," she said quietly. "It's going to be all right."

And then, realizing it was true the moment she said it, "I have a plan."

Grimsley's bravery had given her the final piece of the puzzle. She remembered something else the Lady had told her. "All creatures have the ability to wage battle against the darkest parts of themselves and win. But this battle is too difficult for most to bear. It is far easier to give in, especially when something is forcing those feelings to the forefront."

Grimsley had just overcome the man's influence to come to her aid. If he had done it, the others could too. She couldn't do it for them; they had to fight their own battles. But maybe she could give them a little help.

She turned to face the crowd. "Did everyone see that?" she shouted. She knew some of them were too far gone to hear her, but she had to try.

"Most of you know Grimsley's afraid of just about everything. But I'm here to tell you that even though that's true, he's also incredibly brave."

Several of the Guardians had paused, their fists still raised, and were gaping at her in disbelief.

"Yeah, you heard me," she went on. "He didn't run when a dragon was chasing us down. He didn't hide when we walked into the middle of a war in Downingsburg. And when this guy showed up," she pointed at John Doe, "he tried to make me stay home. So he could protect me."

She pointed at the trembling rabbit.

"Being brave doesn't mean you're not scared. It means being scared but doing what you're supposed to do anyway. He's absolutely terrified, but he just put his body between me and the man, and that's about the bravest thing I've ever seen."

Grimsley had been staring at the ground when she started talking, but by the time she had finished his head was up, and his eyes were on Annie. Slowly he stood up and stepped outside the climbing structure. His knees were knocking so hard against each other that he had to hold onto Annie's hands to get his balance, but he stayed on his feet.

She squeezed his paws tightly in her own and whispered, "Keep fighting, Grim. You have to keep fighting."

Annie scanned the crowd until she found Harold the dragon, who had lifted the terrified prince in his front claws and was lowering him towards his open jaws. She raced across the playground and punched him in the shoulder.

Annie felt a thrill of terror when he looked down at her; nothing of the Harold she knew was visible in his savage face.

"Harold," she said urgently. "You. Are. A. Vegetarian."

Something in his eyes flickered for a moment, and Annie knew the real Harold was still in there.

"You have lived outside the village of Grimm for years, and you have never so much as nibbled on a maiden. You'd much rather have a salad in your cave, or a tea party with Mr. Bear. You are a nice dragon."

At the mention of Mr. Bear, Harold's wings drooped. He put the prince down and shook his giant head as if trying to clear it from sleep. When his eyes settled on Annie again, she recognized her friend.

"Fight," she whispered.

He nodded, and the prince reached out and took his enormous forepaw in his tiny hand.

She pushed her way out into the crowd, moving from creature to creature and reminding them of everything she loved about them. As soon as she saw the light dawn in their eyes, she gave them the same mission she had given Grimsley and Harold. Fight.

And they did fight. As she continued to make her way around the playground, she could see them, turning to their neighbors and helping them find their way back to who they really were. Their determination moved like a wave through the crowd, and Annie watched as one by one they began to believe that she could win. That they could win.

When Annie had spoken to everyone she knew, she returned to the center of the playground to face the man once more.

John Doe was no longer smiling. His expression was blank and empty as a doll's. When Annie met his eyes, however, she saw the fury behind them, and the disbelief. He truly hadn't imagined that anyone could resist him.

"So, this is what I just figured out," she said to him. "All this time, I've been thinking a hero was someone who always knew what to do. That's the way heroes always act in books.

But here's the thing. This isn't a book - this is my life. I don't have any special powers. I don't know how to use a sword. And I don't always do the right thing, even when I know what it is.

Sometimes I get scared," she looked at Grimsley and smiled. "But being scared doesn't mean I can't be brave. And just because I'm not really a hero doesn't mean I can't help people."

John Doe laughed suddenly. "Yes, you've done a wonderful job with that, haven't you, my dear? He looked pointedly out at the bruised and bleeding crowd.

Annie smiled. "I'm not perfect. I don't always know exactly what to do," she said. "But I try. And I'll keep on trying. And you know what else? Another thing I figured out is that being a hero doesn't mean you have to do everything by yourself. I have help. I have friends."

She gestured at Jay and Grimsley.

"And together? We're really strong."

She spread her arms wide to include the crowd, which had been slowly advancing while she spoke, until they stood behind her like an immovable wall.

"We're stronger than you."

Annie turned to face the citizens of the world she had made, and they looked back at her, every face fierce with pride. They were fighting. For her. For Bibylonia. For themselves.

Annie had thought when she first saw her garden that it was the most beautiful thing in the world. She had been wrong.

Jay took a few steps forward and murmured, "Look."

John Doe was still standing exactly where he had been - he hadn't moved an inch. But, was it her imagination, or did he seem somehow lighter than he had before?

She looked closer; she definitely wasn't imagining it. She could actually see through him to the fence on the other side of the playground. As she watched in amazement, he continued to fade until the outline of his form was barely visible, like an overexposed photograph. His legs gave way and he dropped to his knees in the dirt. His wide, shocked eyes met Annie's one last time as he toppled forward and was gone.

For a few long moments, nobody moved. Then the unicorn stepped forward to nose the ground before also fading away, leaving the ground littered with the crumbling remains of the carousel horse it once had been.

CHAPTER 48
THE WATCHER REVEALED

The playground was library quiet. After a few long minutes, Queen Merriweather crawled out from under the climbing structure. At a glance from the queen, the pirates who had been designated as judges swaggered over to where the man had been standing and crouched down, studying the ground thoughtfully. They bent their heads together, arms around each other's shoulders while they conferred. Then they straightened, and one of them signaled to the queen with an emphatic thumbs-up.

Merriweather's smile was ferocious. "The contest has been concluded," she shouted. "John Doe, whatever's left of him, is hereby banished to the Grey Plains, never to return."

Grabbing Annie by the hand, she yanked her arm into the sky. "All hail Miss Annie!"

The playground exploded with sound. Everyone was shouting at once. Harold was breathing fire in great, colorful blasts. The wood elves swarmed the climbing structure like children on the first warm day of spring. Clarence lifted a giggling Bob out of his wheelchair with the end of his powerful tail and paraded him through the crowd.

Annie lost track of the number of hands (and paws) she was asked to shake. No sooner would someone move away than another would step forward to take their place. After the first fifteen or twenty she started to feel like her face might crack from smiling for so long.

She craned her neck to see around a group of ice giants who were dancing a jig with the pirates, hoping to locate Jay and Grimsley. Finally, she spotted them struggling through the crowd towards her.

"Excuse me," she said to the troll who had just asked for her autograph, "but I see my Guardian looking for me."

When she reached them, there was a moment when none of them were exactly sure what to say. They just stood grinning at each other like fools.

It was Jay who broke the silence. "That was absolutely awful. I hated it. I still feel like I'm going to puke. When can I come back?" he asked.

She burst out laughing, throwing her arms around both of them at once.

She felt a hand on her shoulder, and she reluctantly let go of her friends. Queen Merriweather was standing there, an enormous grin on her face, and the black squirrel on her shoulder.

"Told ya you could do it, kid," the queen said, winking at her. She reached into her pocket, took out the wad of gum she had been chewing before the contest and tucked it back into her mouth. Annie tried not to gag.

The squirrel leapt down and landed on the ground in front of Annie. As it soared through the air, the squirrel's body suddenly changed, stretching impossibly into the shape of a woman. A woman with long white hair and wise old eyes.

The Lady.

Every creature on the playground dropped to their knees, even the queen. The Lady smiled and motioned with her gnarled hand for them to rise.

"I knew there was something weird about that squirrel," Annie said.

The Lady laughed. Unlike the man's laugh, which made you want to climb into a hole and never come out again, the Lady's was like a child's, joyful and uncomplicated.

"I rather enjoy being a squirrel," she said merrily. "One gets to see a lot of the world from the treetops. And people do some very interesting things when they think no one is looking."

"You've been following me ever since I first got here," Annie realized. "I kept thinking I was seeing different squirrels, but it was always you, wasn't it?"

The Lady nodded.

Annie paused, wanting to choose her next words carefully.

"So, I guess the thing I don't understand is…you knew what he was capable of, better than anyone. And if you were following me, you knew I wasn't doing such a great job fighting him. Clarence almost killed Bob, and I barely managed to stop it. Why didn't you do anything to help me?"

Annie couldn't quite keep the frustration out of her voice as she said this.

The Lady's peaceful expression didn't change as she replied, "Because you did not need my help."

Annie's mouth fell open. "What do you mean, I didn't need help? I totally needed help! If I hadn't thought of using the clock-keeper's cane to get Clarence out of there…"

"You are making my point for me, child."

The old woman took Annie's hands in her own.

"When you first entered Bibylonia, I asked the forest to give you what you needed to aid you on your journey, and it did. It dressed you in comfortable clothes. And it provided you with tools to help you in your endeavors."

"My pouch." Annie's hand went to it automatically.

"Indeed," she smiled. "My instructions to the forest were very clear – you were to receive what you needed while in our world. You decided how to use what you were given. Another person might have made different choices when presented with a furious dragon, or a stubborn wood elf. But you looked always for what you could do that would help the most people and harm the fewest. It was that, more than anything the pouch provided, that made you a hero to those who live here."

"But," Annie was confused. "I didn't even use the pouch to help Clarence when he attacked Bob. It never even occurred to me."

"Nor did you use it today when you faced down the man and won the day. You didn't need magical help to save Clarence, or to defeat John Doe. You managed that with your own quick wits. And in the end," she smiled at Annie, "you were brave enough to do what needed to be done. I would have done you a disservice if I had tried to rescue you."

Annie was quiet for a moment, processing that information. If she looked back at the events of the past few days, she could admit, if only to herself, that she had been pretty brave, especially if you knew how terrified she had felt on the inside. She wished she knew how to be that brave back home.

The Lady seemed to know what Annie was thinking. "Remember what I said before, child. People are the same, wherever they might be."

"But I don't know how to be that girl anywhere but here," she said hopelessly, thinking of the twins and the trapped feeling she got whenever it was time to go to school.

The Lady smiled. "There is only one way to become the person you want to be, my dear. You must simply be that person, as often as you can, and a little more each day."

And with that, she released Annie's hands and turned to walk away.

"Wait!" Annie called after her.

The Lady stopped and looked back at her.

"How could you do it?" Annie asked.

"How could I leave the safety of your world, as well as my own, in the hands of an eleven-year-old girl? Is that what you want to know?"

Annie was beyond being surprised at how the old woman seemed to know her mind. She simply nodded.

"Because I know you, Anneliese Marie Albright. And because I know what John Doe did not, which is that sometimes the parts of ourselves we most despise can actually make us stronger. You are brave not despite your fear, but because of it. You could not crave fairness as much as you do if you didn't carry the burden of those times you have not been fair, or kind. Because of this, you have wisdom in you that many grown people never manage to achieve."

"I am in a unique position to know how much, of course," the Lady said, with a rather mischievous smile. "After all, you created me."

This time, when she walked away, Annie found herself completely at a loss for words.

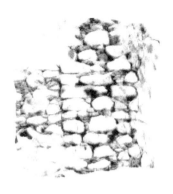

CHAPTER 49
BACK TO THE GARDEN

Jay talked non-stop all the way back to the garden. Annie didn't mind. She was still thinking through the events of the day and Jay's running monologue meant she wasn't really expected to participate in the conversation.

"...so I guess I would have expected John Doe to look, I don't know, scarier than that," Jay was saying. "He mostly just looked like a regular guy. Although," he continued thoughtfully, "that is consistent with some predatory species in the animal kingdom. For example, a platypus looks friendly, but they're venomous. You would never think of them as dangerous until it was too late."

People in the real world were like that too, Annie thought. Beau and Ashley came to mind, of course, with their angelic faces, but then she thought about others, people she had seen on the news or read about in books. The most terrible villains in history had all worn ordinary human faces. The fact that you couldn't look at them and see that they were monsters only made them more dangerous.

Annie looked over at Grimsley, who was watching Jay with a mixture of confusion and amusement. She felt a sudden surge of gratitude; no matter which world she was in, she had the very best friends.

When they reached the ruins of Annie's garden wall, they found the Guardians already at work gathering up the fallen stones and mixing mortar to cement them back into place. Several of them raised their hands in greeting as they approached, and the cyclops thumped Grimsley fondly across the shoulders. Annie and Jay caught him before he fell.

Annie was relieved to feel the chain mail fall away as they passed through the gate. Hopefully she'd never need it again.

They spent the next several hours cleaning up the garden. Jay and Grimsley spent most of that time clearing debris while Annie helped to rebuild the wall, painstakingly applying cement between the stones and carefully lowering them into place.

The sun was setting in Bibylonia when she put down her trowel at last. Her arms ached and her legs were trembling from the effort of lifting the heavy stones. It was a good feeling, though, knowing that her muscles were sore from helping make things right.

She stepped back to inspect the wall. It wasn't as perfect as it had been; there were cracks in some of the stones, and the mortar looked lumpy in places. But as she stood watching, ivy began to wind its way up the wall. No longer black and poisonous looking, it flowed gently over the stones, curling around the bars of the gate. Tiny white flowers sprouted from the vines.

She felt something tugging at the back of her shoe and turned around to find a tiny patch of neon yellow irises at her feet. When she bent down to get a better look, they skittered away across the path, giggling.

All around her, the rest of the garden was coming back to life. Buds exploded from the trees' barren branches, and green shoots speckled the ground as plants forced their way up to the sun. It might take a little time, but the garden would find its way to what it was supposed to be.

Just like she would.

"I'll be back tomorrow night," Annie called, even though the Guardians had already returned home. She knew the forest could hear her, even if they couldn't. "To finish cleaning up the rest of Bibylonia."

A light wind lifted Annie's hair. She smiled.

"I'll see you soon," she said, hugging Grimsley tightly.

He hugged her back. "I will be waiting, Miss Annie. Always."

Annie pushed open the door that would take them home.

CHAPTER 50
BACK TO SCHOOL

Just before she opened the door it had occurred to her to wonder how it would know to take them back to school rather than to Annie's house. But the magic of the garden didn't let her down, and they found the nurse's office, luckily empty, on the other side.

She looked over at Jay, who was already sitting up, looking as groggy as anyone waking up from a nap in the middle of the day.

Just then, the nurse came bustling in to check on them. "Feeling a little better, are we?" she asked distractedly, rifling through a drawer and gathering up a pile of bandages and antiseptic. Groans of pain issued from outside the door.

Annie glanced at the clock. Even though they'd been in Bibylonia for hours, it appeared to be the same time here as when they left. She decided to take advantage of the nurse's preoccupation to make their escape.

"I've still got a headache, but I think I can go back to class," she said, stepping on Jay's foot as inconspicuously as she could.

"Ow! Um, yes, me too," he said, feebly.

Fortunately, the nurse wasn't paying attention. She told them vaguely to sign themselves out before hurrying back out of the room to tend to the injured boys.

Neither of them spoke as they walked, but it was a comfortable silence. At the door to their classroom their eyes met for a moment. Annie could tell Jay was thinking the same thing she was - how strange it was to be returning to an ordinary day after what they'd just been through. The fact that they had to go to PE after they had just saved the world seemed completely unfair.

When the bell rang at the end of the day, Annie got up quickly and started helping Jay gather up his belongings, a habit formed from weeks of trying to beat the twins to the bus line. She paused in the middle of stuffing folders into his backpack and slowly put them back down on the desk. Jay looked at her quizzically.

"Take your time," she told him. "It's not like the bus is even here yet."

By the time they made it outside, Beau and Ashley were already there, holding court as usual. Jay and Annie dropped their bags on the ground and sat down on the sidewalk. Annie pulled a book out of her bag, flipped it open and started to read.

After only a few paragraphs, she heard Ashley's girlish giggle cut through the chatter. Even though she had been expecting it since they sat down, it still made her teeth clench.

"Oh, look," Ashley called out, "it's Jane and Andy."

The twins' little gang howled with laughter.

Looking around, Annie noticed that most of the other kids in the line weren't laughing, but they were all watching to see what would happen next. She remembered something her mother had said when her little sister had pulled all the books off her bookshelf for the five-hundredth time. She had told Annie that the best thing to do to get Maisy to stop was to simply walk away. Without anyone to react to her behavior, it wouldn't be as fun for her anymore.

Beau and Ashley were looking for a reaction too. Walking away from the bus stop wasn't an option, but if they didn't get the kind of reaction they were expecting from Jay and Annie, maybe no one would be interested in watching, not even the twins themselves.

She thought about the expression on John Doe's face when he realized that she wasn't afraid anymore, that he had lost control of the battle. She needed to find a way to show the twins that she wasn't afraid of them, either.

It only took her a few moments to decide how to do it. Her stomach felt like it was full of wriggling worms, but she was determined. It was time to be the person she wanted to be, all the time.

Annie scooted closer to Jay and bumped him in the leg. He looked up from his book, startled. She winked at him, and grinned. His eyes widened but then he caught on, smiling with her as if he was in on the joke.

"Sorry," Annie said brightly in response to Ashley's obvious confusion. "I just remembered something funny."

She looked back down at her book, pretending to read. And waited.

It didn't take long. Ashley was unaccustomed to anyone ignoring her, and she clearly didn't like it. When she spoke again, her voice was noticeably snippier than usual.

"What's so funny, Andy? Something in your dorky book? Or are you thinking about the look on Jane's face when she 'fell' out of her swing the other day? Because I thought that was hilarious too."

Jay's shoulders slumped slightly, but Annie nudged him hard with her knee.

"Oh," she said lightly, "you mean when you pushed Jay out of the swing? No, I didn't really think that was funny. My baby sister does things like that all the time. It's super annoying, but my mom says she'll grow out of it eventually."

She tried not to grin as Ashley's lip curled into a snarl.

Jay snorted. A handful of people in the crowd wore tentative smiles, as if they weren't sure exactly what was happening, but had high hopes for whatever was coming next.

"Actually, I was thinking about something my dad told me the other day, about your old school," she went on.

Ashley stared at her.

"Oh," she said, "did you not know my dad works for the school district? He takes care of all the computer stuff, you know, like the attendance records, grades, student transfer files, stuff like that."

It was a guess on Annie's part. The twins spent a lot of time talking about things they had done to kids at their previous school. It was an easy way to build up their reputations, since student records were protected. They could tell as many horrible stories as they wanted, and no one could ever prove they weren't true.

She thought of Harold, hiding his gentle heart behind a fearsome, fire-breathing façade. And of the queen, insulting John Doe so no one would see how terrified she was. In both cases their rude behavior was like a mask they wore to protect themselves from harm. That didn't mean she thought the twins were secretly great people, but she thought that maybe, just maybe, they hadn't been entirely honest about the reason they had transferred in the middle of the year.

Of course, her father hadn't really told her anything. But they didn't have any way to know that.

One glance in their direction told Annie her instincts had been good. Ashley was looking at her brother anxiously. When she sensed Annie watching her, she jerked her head quickly back around. For the first time, Annie saw wariness as well as malice in her face.

She gave Ashley another big smile, and then shifted position so that her back was towards the twins, bending her head towards her book. She knew that wouldn't be the end of it, but she thought it was a pretty good start.

CHAPTER 51
FAMILY

Jay and Annie sat in the middle of the bus that afternoon the way they used to, talking in low voices about the events of the day. Occasionally one of them would laugh out loud at the memory of dancing ice giants, or how Harold had tried to push Clarence in one of the swings. That hadn't ended well. Annie had spent so much time the past few weeks just trying to survive the ride home from school, she had forgotten how much she looked forward to it - this time with her best friend.

When the bus reached her stop, she bumped Jay's shoulder with her backpack. "I'll email you later."

She stood on the sidewalk and watched his grinning face through the window until the bus pulled away and out of sight.

Looking down the street towards her house, she saw her dad's car in the driveway. Suddenly, it was all she could do to walk, instead of run, to her front door. After everything that had happened, she was desperate to see her family.

She was only about halfway up the driveway when she heard the screaming. Panicked, she ran the rest of the way up the hill, frantically shrugging her bookbag off her shoulders. She dropped it on the doormat and pushed the door open.

There, in the center of the living room, stood Maisy, playing cards scattered across the carpet at her feet. Her face was purple with rage, and the amount of noise she was making could probably have woken a goblin. Her dad stood in the doorway that led from the living room into the kitchen, his cell phone in his hand and a resigned expression on his face.

Her heart leapt at the sight of them, alive, safe, and completely unaware that their world had been invaded just a few hours before.

She stepped back out onto the front porch, grabbing her bag and dumping it in the hallway. "Go back to work, Dad," she said, smiling. "I got this."

She walked over and started to pick up the cards.

Her dad looked at her strangely for a moment. Annie wasn't too surprised by that. She hadn't been much of a team player lately. That was going to change.

Annie sat down on the floor in front of her sister. She shuffled the cards quickly and started dealing out a hand of Old Maid.

Maisy was still crying, but she watched curiously while Annie laid out the cards in two neat little piles.

"You ready?" Annie asked her.

Maisy promptly closed her mouth and sat down hard on the carpet.

Annie played with her sister until Maisy lost interest in the game and started throwing her cards up in the air whenever it was her turn. Usually when this happened Annie got irritated and walked away. Today, however, she threw hers up in the air as well. Her sister looked at her appraisingly for a moment before picking up another handful of cards, this time tossing them directly at Annie. They were still throwing cards at each other and laughing when her mother walked in the door from work ten minutes later.

Annie's homework seemed much tougher than usual that evening, due to her inattentiveness in class the past few weeks. When she finally finished and went back downstairs, her dad was helping Maisy into her pajamas, and her mother was curled up on the sofa next to a tall stack of books with library stickers on them.

Annie picked up the first book on the pile. She sat down and kissed her mother on the cheek. Her mother's arm circled her shoulders, pulling her close.

"You all right, Annie?" her mother asked softly.

"I'm fine, Mom," she answered truthfully, for the first time in weeks. She picked up the book on the top of the pile and handed it to her mother. "Do you think maybe you could read to me tonight?"

CHAPTER 52
THE PATH FORWARD

The rebuilding of Bibylonia took several weeks. Some of the windows in Aesoppla's town hall had been broken during the chess match, someone had set a fire in Rapunzel's tower, and the wood elves had sustained significant damage to their forest home from sheltering all the citizens of Bibylonia from John Doe. Ice giants do not make good houseguests.

Annie went from town to town, helping wherever she could. She went on foot, because Marty had never again materialized with her in the garden. The Lady said that was because she didn't need a talisman anymore. Maybe that was true, but she definitely could have used a ride.

She, Harold and the villagers of Grimm spent an afternoon cleaning soot off the walls in the tower. Harold had gotten to know a number of the townspeople after the teddy bear theft. Apparently once they realized he wasn't going to eat any of them, they became much more friendly. Annie watched the volunteers come and go all day, but she never caught sight of Cinderella.

Grimsley traveled with her whenever he could. Since the Battle of the Meadow, he was getting a lot more respect from the other Guardians, and he often found himself recruited these days for special security details, and even occasional sporting events.

Today, he and Annie were on their way back to the garden from a long day clearing fallen trees around the wood elves' encampment. They were tired and walking a lot more slowly than usual.

"We're almost done," she said, stretching her sore arms over her head. "Soon everything will be like it was before."

"No, Miss Annie. I don't think it will ever be like it was before."

She thought about the mended spots on her garden wall, and the faint

162

smell of smoke that still lingered in Rapunzel's tower. No, even though they had repaired most of the damage, they couldn't erase what had happened, any more than Annie could herself go back to the way she had been before.

"Hey, Grim," she said, reluctantly. "I don't think I'm going to be able to come every night anymore, at least not for a while."

Grimsley's ears drooped.

"I talked about it with the Lady," she went on, "and she says I should be able to control it now, so that I come only when I want to, not every time I fall asleep.

It isn't that I don't want to come," she said. "But I need to figure out how to live in my world too. And I need to get better at controlling what I bring into this one, so I don't ever put anyone in danger again. The Lady says she can teach me. But it's going to take some time."

"Perhaps," he said thoughtfully, "when you are not here, I can use the map myself to find those who are in need of assistance. After all, I am a Guardian."

He puffed his chest out but overbalanced and almost knocked Annie over.

She pushed back on his paws to right him, grinning.

"That is a fantastic idea, Grim," she said, and she meant it. "Bibylonia would be lucky to have a hero like you. Maybe you could ask Lady Cottontail if she'd like to come along? After all, it's her map."

Grimsley's ears twitched.

"Maybe the next time you come," he said hurriedly, changing the subject, "you can bring Jay with you. I'm sure the Lady would allow it, since he has been here before."

"I'll ask him," Annie smiled.

"Or," he went on, "when she is older, you could bring your sister."

"If you had seen what she did to one of my stuffed animals, you definitely wouldn't be inviting my sister. Let's just say I like your ears on your head and leave it at that."

Annie laughed at the horrified expression on Grimsley's face.

They stopped a few feet away from the garden gate. The rust had been carefully scraped away, and the iron gleamed in the afternoon sun.

"I'll see you really soon," she said, through the lump in her throat.

"Until then, Miss Annie," he said, with a bow so deep that his ears brushed the ground.

He walked away into the forest. She watched him until he disappeared into the trees.

Turning back to the gate, she pulled out her key and opened the heavy iron door. It had been a long day. She was ready to go home.

ABOUT THE AUTHOR

Heather Primm lives in Durham, NC, with her husband, two of their children, three cats, a rat, and eight chickens. When she's not writing, she can usually be found in the kitchen making a colossal mess, complaining about the weeds in the garden (but not actually doing anything about them) or helping someone in the house find something that's lying about in plain sight.

Made in the USA
Middletown, DE
30 June 2022

68139904R00099